LUCKY 13

Life Lessons Learned The Hard Way

By

Bobby Bland

E BOOK: 978-1-966131-46-5

PAPERBACK: 978-1-966131-47-2

HARDCOVER: 978-1-966131-48-9

Published by **Author Publications**: 2025

https://www.authorpublications.com

+1 (771) 203-5560

Printed in the United States of America

Dedication

For my family, particularly my Grandkids—Cataleya, Hadley, Henry, Corinne, Gabriel, and Genevieve. I wish all of you a life full of God's blessings and lessons learned. You make me very happy.

- Papa

Acknowledgment

Special appreciation to Emily Amadon for her help with this book. Not only did she write the Prologue and assist in writing Chapter 7 about the Snack Lab experience, but she also lived the experience with me for the last 9 years! I couldn't have made it without her!

Thanks to Amy and her crew of the Bentonville (Dodson Street) Heroes Coffee. Thanks for the hospitality and great Green Tea while I wrote the book!

Special thanks to my wife, Debbie, who allowed me to spend all that time at the coffee shop bringing this book to life!

Appreciation to all the guests and customers I have helped and served over the years at Food 4 Less, Price Chopper in Oklahoma, Village Insurance, and Snack Lab. You have given my work purpose and challenged me in every way. I thank all of you.

Special thanks to Kirk Dupps, who taught me more about retail than all the books ever did!

Thank you to Doug Bachman and Village Insurance, who offered me the opportunity to be a part of the organization for 20 years.

I am grateful for all three of our children, who have taught me more about life than I ever could have taught them. They have grown into fantastic human beings, and I am honored to have been a part of seeing them grow.

I owe a great deal to my sister, Belynda Bland, for all her help and support over the years, particularly when we were kids. Thanks for all the times you drove me to A&W for a Root Beer Float.

I would be remiss if I didn't include a special thank you to my mom and dad, Mary and Bob Bland. God blessed me with two of the very best people I have ever known. I was close to both in entirely different ways, but they both were loving and caring and taught me life lessons I will never forget.

About the Author

Bobby Bland and his wife, Debbie, are rare natives of Northwest Arkansas. Raised in Rogers, Bobby graduated from The University of Arkansas with a degree in Marketing and an MBA from U of A.

In 45 years in the business world, Bobby has maintained his focus on one thing—the customer. His management experience includes:

- 2 years as a grocery sales specialist.

- 13 years working in Merchandising for (Food 4 Less stores) and Walmart Supercenters.

- 1 year as President/CEO of Price Marts in Oklahoma

- 20 years serving as Commercial Sales Manager and later Vice President of Village Insurance and Commercial Risk Service.

- After a life-changing journey that turned his health around, Bland decided to sell his ownership in Village Insurance and earned his certifications as a Certified Health Coach and Life Coach. Bobby focuses on helping his clients lead healthy lifestyles with quality foods for their daily routine and active lifestyles filled with exercise and adventures.

- This coaching journey also led Bobby to the idea of Snack Lab, a hybrid Health food store/Healthy Restaurant/Healthy grab-n-go store. With partner Emily Amadon, they operated the stores for 7 ½ year, and just recently sold.

In addition to his passion for improving the health of people in Northwest Arkansas, Bland's other interests include:

- Spending time with their 6 Grandkids
- Hiking to any mountain peaks in Colorado
- Singing and praising God
- Anything Razorbacks

Table of Contents

Foreword

Asking someone to be your business partner is not a casual question. A business partnership requires an immense amount of time, trust, and commitment. It's not a decision to take lightly if you intend to truly build something special.

I first met Bobby in 2008. His daughter, Anna, and I both chose to venture from our comforts of Northwest Arkansas to Baylor University for our college experience. We didn't really know each other "back home." However, we quickly became friends as we bravely navigated the new world of college away from familiarities. How serendipitous that the Lord would use a dear college friendship in Central Texas to eventually lead to a business partnership back home in Northwest Arkansas.

Bobby and I were business partners for 9 years, which you'll read more about in chapter seven. In our quest to grow (and survive) our business, there were many days we saw each other more than our families. This gave me a front row seat to learning *from* Bobby and *with* Bobby. I can confidently say, I couldn't have had a better business partner. He is a man of conviction, moral character, loyalty, and steadfast love.

He and I are different people today than when we agreed to be business partners in 2015. But that's the thing about life, right? A life well lived is always open to change, to learning, to growing. It's what you do with life's lessons that really makes a difference, and Bobby has always endeavored to make something of his life's lessons.

The chapters in this book are Bobby's life lessons, most of which did not come easy. His personal anecdotes and stories help these lessons come to life. I challenge you to take Bobby's stories and let them inspire you to grow, to learn, to love. If even one of these stories resonates and impacts you, I believe you'll be better for it. I'll never forget the time one of our staff members looked me dead in the eye and said, "You're nice and all but I like hanging around Bobby because he is a special kind of person." It's wise to find special people around you to learn from. Take these stories, learn from them, and then go out into the world and put them into practice. You never know how these lessons may impact you, and maybe someone else in the future.

Emily Amadon

Introduction

I was born and raised in Rogers, Arkansas, a place that defined my childhood with sports, family, hard work, and an early love for the Arkansas Razorbacks. Growing up in middle-class small-town America, my parents worked tirelessly and instilled values of doing the right thing—though, admittedly, I didn't always follow their advice!

The greatest blessing of my life came when I met Debbie, my wife of nearly 42 years. Debbie is the most incredible person I know—caring, funny, and beautiful inside and out. I would be nothing without her love and support. I once saw a poster listing the "23 Most Important Things for a Happy Life." Number 1 was "Marry the right person," and number 2 read, "If you don't get #1 right, none of the others matter." That couldn't be more true in my life.

Together, Debbie and I have built a wonderful life, blessed with our three children: Jesse, John, and Anna. Watching them grow into remarkable adults- all with college degrees and all with amazing spouses—fills me with pride. Most importantly, they are incredible human beings. Today, my greatest joy revolves around our six grandchildren: Cataleya, Hadley, Henry, Corinne, Genevieve, and

Gabriel—the youngest two being twins. God's blessings in my life are countless, and my family tops the list.

As a child, I loved to read, particularly about famous figures—world leaders, movie stars, and, of course, athletes. While I spent much of my time outdoors playing sports, I also made time to dive into stories about real people. Their journeys, challenges, and triumphs captivated me, far more than fictional tales ever could. Back then, TV offered only one college football game per week—hard to imagine now!—but it left plenty of time for reading and dreaming about the possibilities life could hold.

After earning my undergraduate degree and MBA in Arkansas, I embarked on a diverse business career. From working in the grocery industry and commercial insurance to co-founding Snack Lab, a fresh concept with my friend Emily Amadon, my professional life has been anything but dull. Along the way, I've pursued my passions outside the business world, too.

I had the privilege of coaching youth sports—football, softball, baseball, and basketball—for over 18 years, not just for my kids but for countless others. Those years taught me as much as I taught the kids. I also explored my love of music by recording two solo Contemporary Christian albums and even published a book, *ABC's of Christmas Prayers.*

Now, at 67, I look back on a life filled with blessings and lessons learned—some of them the hard way. My hope is to share those lessons with you, offering insights to enhance your life and deepen your faith.

The Beginning of 13

I was born on June 13, 1957—a date that seemed to set the stage for a lifelong connection with the number 13. From my earliest memories, the number has followed me, appearing in the most unexpected and meaningful ways.

The favorite memories from my childhood all revolved around one thing…Arkansas Razorback Football. My parents, both Arkansas natives, were devoted Razorback fans. They didn't have any kids at the time, so my dad only bought 2 tickets. By 1953, my older sister was born, so the next season Dad bought 4 season tickets. I guess he knew I was coming sooner or later, but little did he know how much I would grow to love the Hogs! I attended my first Razorback game in 1960 at just three years old, sitting in

Section 3, Row 13, Seats 13–16. Even at that age, the number 13 was quietly weaving its way into my story. I can't recall many details from those early games, but I remember the excitement of being there with my family. Over the years, those seats became a family tradition. Fast forward to today—75 years later—and my family and I are still in the same spot. Now called Section 103, Row 13, Seats 13–16, those seats represent so much more than just a place to watch football; they are a testament to family, loyalty, and tradition.

My Lucky Number

When I turned seven, I was finally old enough to play Little League baseball. With 12 kids on the team, each player was assigned a number from 1 to 12. But I was a big kid— much bigger than the others—and the jerseys didn't fit me. My coach had to get a special jersey made just for me, and what number did it have? You guessed it—#13. That number became my constant companion throughout my baseball career, from Little League to high school. It was only fitting that I played baseball for 13 years.

Football, however, was a different story. As a lineman, #13 wasn't an option, so I had to leave my lucky number behind for that chapter of my life.

Why 13?

Hopefully, you will find this book about more than just about number 13, or I will lose your attention quickly. I want you to consume this book in pieces- 13 of them (Woops, there's that number again!). I really want to leave you thinking- contemplating how you can make your life have more meaning and adventure. Each of the 13 things I have learned are full of promise, but also pain and disappointment.

At the end of each chapter, you'll find a section called *Food 4 Thought*. These reflective prompts include thought-provoking questions designed to guide your personal growth or spark discussions in a group setting. I've also included writings—some my own, others from people whose words have inspired me.

My Hope for You

This book is more than a collection of ideas; it's an invitation to reflect on your own journey, a self-realization.

I hope my stories will resonate with you and inspire you to embrace meaning and adventure in your life. My ultimate wish is that my children, grandchildren, and maybe even yours will find something here to unlock their potential. Who knows? Maybe they'll even discover 13 things that will change their lives.

Chapter 1
Do Unto Others

I was walking into a building the other day, and there was a lady in front of me. As we approached the door, she opened it and held it for me. Wait — that's not right! I said, "After you," and she retorted, "You go ahead." I was confused for a moment, then it hit me: she held the door because I'M OLD! I was taught to hold the door for ladies and older people, and now she was doing it for an old guy! I didn't know whether to be thankful or offended.

The first and possibly most important lesson I have learned and affirmed in my life is **The Golden Rule**:

Matthew 7:12: "In everything, do unto others as you would have them do unto you."

My dad pounded that phrase into my head as a kid. But more importantly, he lived it every day. I recently spoke at the memorial service for Jane Ann Bales McBride, one of my cousins in South Arkansas. Her daughter handed me an article that Jane Ann had saved for years. The article, published in the Arkansas Game & Fish Commission magazine, was my dad's recollection of growing up in the "Big Woods" of Dallas County, Arkansas, during the Depression. His father was one of the first Game and Fish Wardens in Arkansas, and their family lived in the middle of those woods. One of the final things my dad said in that article caught my attention: "All of my parents' efforts that I remember were directed towards education, conservation, preservation, and practicing the Golden Rule."

As you can see, the Golden Rule was a family tradition.

Lessons from Childhood

It wasn't until I started reading the Bible consistently that I found out this principle was from God's Word. It meant even more to me after that. The actual phrase was spoken by Jesus during His Sermon on the Mount. Later in Matthew 7:13-14, Jesus added:

"Enter through the narrow gate. For wide is the gate and broad is the road that leads to destruction, and many enter through it. But small is the gate and narrow the road that leads to life, and only a few find it."

Lesson #1: Treat others as you want to be treated.

As a kid, I was bigger than anyone in my class. I wasn't fat—just "big-boned!" I was proud of being the biggest kid in class, a full head taller than everyone else. But that didn't stop some kids from teasing me about being different. That's all it takes, isn't it? Just be different, and you'll hear about it. My mom told me not to worry about it. She said something that stuck with me throughout my life:

"Making fun of others or calling them names is a sign of weakness, not strength. Just remember not to do the same thing to others."

Bullying isn't just a childhood issue; it extends into adulthood and often leads to devastating consequences. I have seen this attitude all my life: You can rarely go a full week without hearing about a mass shooting somewhere in this country. Mass shootings at schools, churches, businesses and public places. Many of these shootings can be traced to the shooter being bullied as a child or adult. Children can be mean but guess what! So can adults. Parents, teach your children that how we treat others matters. Let's bring back the Golden Rule.

The Golden Rule in Business

Contrary to popular jokes, the Golden Rule is NOT: *"He who has the gold makes the rules!"*

The Golden Rule applies in the business world just as much as it does in personal life. Over the past 45 years, I've run and helped run several businesses, and I've found that treating others the way you want to be treated should be the #1 goal of any organization. This applies to both customers and employees.

If you treat your team members with respect and dignity, they will, in turn, treat your customers the same way. Here's an example: Have you ever gone into a restaurant 10 minutes before it closes? How were you treated? Did the servers sigh in disgust and make you move your chair while they mopped, or did they smile and make you feel welcome? Here's the difference:

• Servers who dislike late guests are often focused on their own inconvenience.
• Servers who welcome late guests have learned gratitude and know their attitude improves the customer experience.

However, a practical note: arriving right before closing is not ideal. The cooks in the kitchen might not be as thrilled as the servers—and remember, they're preparing your food!

****

A Verse from "Always Stay Humble & Kind" by Tim McGraw:

"Don't take for granted the love this life gives you
When you get where you're going don't forget turn back around
And help the next one in line
Always stay humble and kind."

****

Empathy in Immigration

Immigration has been a contentious issue in the U.S. for decades, intensifying in recent years. As a citizen, I believe it's best if everyone in the U.S. was a legal resident. However, that's not the real world. When we started Snack Lab, my business partner Emily and I didn't plan on hiring illegal immigrants. But as the business grew, our stance changed. We realized the best candidates for kitchen roles were often immigrants. Many came from El Salvador or Mexico, fleeing violence or poverty in their home country. They were hard workers, made it to work without excuses, and for the most part, were the most trusted team members.

These employees were some of the hardest-working and most trustworthy team members we had. A green card doesn't make someone a good employee or a good person. These individuals loved their families, treated others with dignity, and contributed immensely to our business.

What we also found was that unless they married a U.S. citizen, these hard-working family-oriented people didn't have a chance of becoming citizens. The immigration system in this country is broken, but that's no reason to hate the people caught in it. **Put yourself in their shoes. The Golden Rule applies here too.**

A Life Lived by the Golden Rule

My wife Debbie is a shining example of someone who lives out the Golden Rule every day. She has never met a stranger. By the time she finishes a conversation with someone, she knows their birthday, how many kids they have, and more. Everyone she meets feels better than they did before they met Debbie. If you want your children to learn how to live the Golden Rule, let them spend a day with Debbie.

Looking back on my life, I've learned the value of the Golden Rule the hard way many times. We are all God's children, struggling through life together. When we put ourselves above others, humanity begins to rot.

A Call to Action

Let's start a new movement today. Move away from division and negativity. Reject the belief that we improve ourselves by knocking others down. Instead, embrace the timeless wisdom of Jesus:

"Do unto others as you would have them do unto you."

Chapter 1 Food for Thought

1. **<u>Chapter 1 Challenge</u>**: The first person you encounter this week that you wouldn't normally encounter, approach them and talk to them. This could be a person from another country, a person of a different religion, or anything else. Treat them with kindness. Make their day a little better somehow. Honestly, it may totally confuse them! Record your thoughts afterward:

____

____

____

____

____

2. Have you ever had a time when you weren't treated like you thought you should be? How did it make your feel?

____

____

____

____

3. Describe your feelings on immigration and illegal workers in our country:

____

____

____

____

4. What can you do to help with this issue?

____

____

____

____

Chapter 2
But What If...

It was the worst day of my life. Until then, my life had been nothing but positive. I grew up in the sixties and early seventies in Rogers, Arkansas—a small town where neighbors cared for one another. In many ways, it truly was "The Village" that raised me, alongside my middle-class parents. I was a decent athlete, an excellent student, and I cherished every moment of my upbringing. A full athletic scholarship to play college football seemed like the perfect continuation of my story. Life was unfolding beautifully yet humbly.

But losing someone you love is shattering, especially at 21 years old. The pain was overwhelming, and the guilt—

the unshakable feeling that it was somehow my fault—exacerbated that pain. We all cope with loss in our own different ways, but I lacked the tools to steer through this storm. My family, though strong and supportive, had always championed resilience: "Pull yourself up by your bootstraps" was the mantra I often heard, though I was never quite sure what it really meant. Yet, there was a missing element—a deeper spiritual foundation, a connection with God that could have provided solace and strength.

In the aftermath of this loss, I felt completely alone. The weight of my guilt was suffocating, and I tried desperately to press forward, clinging to the only coping mechanisms I knew. I threw myself into work, finished my college studies, and outwardly maintained the illusion that everything was fine. No one suspected the inner whirlwind that was quietly consuming me.

For two years, I lived in a state of denial as if nothing happened, going through the motions but spiraling internally. On the surface, I was functioning—working, finishing college, and partying my guts out. I partied recklessly, often surviving on as little as eight hours of sleep in a **week!** Inside, however, I was falling apart.

Eventually, the façade crumbled. Exhausted and hopeless, I left town, contemplating whether I would ever return—or whether I even wanted to. This ridiculous of a lifestyle finally took its toll.

Somehow, I found myself in a small town in East Texas. I can't remember the journey, but I conspicuously recall pulling into the parking lot of the first church I saw. I didn't know why I was there, but I felt an inexplicable pull, a gentle nudge I couldn't ignore. I stepped inside the sanctuary, sat down, and wept—uncontrollably, for hours. The weight of my grief finally poured out in those tears.

Eventually, the minister noticed me sitting alone and approached. He sat beside me, listened as I shared my pain, and then prayed with me. A saying I have heard all my life is "It's not what happens to you, it's how you handle it." This minister reshaped it a bit, saying:

"The challenge is not what happens to you, but who do you have to lean on to enable you to move forward in your life. The key is to be still and ask God to guide your path."

Those words pierced my heart with its spearing reality, aligning perfectly with a powerful truth I later found in Scripture:

"I have told you these things, so that in me you may have peace. In this world you will have trouble. But take heart! I have overcome the world." (John 16:33)

At that moment, I understood what had been missing—a relationship with a loving, ever-present God. For too long, I had tried to numb my pain through work, academics, and alcohol. Two of those pursuits were productive but ultimately hollow without God, while the third led only to destruction.

Life Lesson #1:

It's not what happens to you that defines your life—it's what you do with it.

When life delivers a critical blow, how do you respond? Do you lash out, seeking vengeance? Do you wallow in self-pity? Or do you look in the mirror and confront the truth? I've done all the above, and let me tell you, the lessons learned without God by your side can be devastating.

In that church, something shifted. The minister's guidance and my tears of surrender marked the beginning of a transformation—a realization that my strength alone was insufficient, but God's strength was more than enough. It wasn't coincidence that brought me to that sanctuary; it was grace. That day, I began to grasp the power of leaning on Him during life's greatest challenges.

7 Rules of Life

1. Make peace with your past so it won't interfere with the present.
2. What others think of you is none of your business.
3. Time heals almost everything—give it time.
4. Don't compare your life to others or judge them; you have no idea what their journey is about.
5. Stop overthinking—it's alright not to know all the answers. God will reveal them in His timing.
6. No one is in charge of your happiness except you.
7. Smile—you don't have to carry the weight of all the world's problems.

It's so easy to look back and wonder, *What if?* Over the past nine years—what I often call "The Era of Snack Lab"—I've learned just how powerful perspective can be. This chapter of my life is a testament to both dreams realized and the lessons hidden in challenges. As a concept, we were wildly acclaimed as it was something unprecedented for Northwest Arkansas or anywhere else, for that matter.

When Emily and I began this journey, we had no guarantees. All we had was a vision: to fill a void in Northwest Arkansas for real, ready-to-eat food—free from processed sugars and preservatives. From this dream, Snack Lab was born. Along the way, we introduced wholesome gluten-free breakfasts and lunches, healthy smoothies, acai bowls, soups, salads, handmade snacks, and even pupusas. Our services grew to include catering, meal plans, family dinners, and prepared lunches for preschools. What started off as a concept quickly became a hit, and we expanded into Rogers and Fayetteville with new locations.

But then came March 2020—the onset of the COVID-19 pandemic. It was a trial we could never have anticipated. Over 40% of restaurants across the country didn't survive the next 18 months, and despite pouring every resource we had into our business, our Rogers and Fayetteville stores succumbed as well. Closing them was heartbreaking. Our Bentonville store barely held on by a thread, but it eventually began to recover as the pandemic receded, becoming a distant memory.

Still, the toll of those years—2020 to 2022—was immense. They drained us financially and, even more so, emotionally.

Questions That Linger

After all the ups and downs of a unique business concept, countless questions arose:

- What if we hadn't added those two locations?
- What if we hadn't been forced to let go of our best team member during a hiring crisis?
- What if we hadn't lost a crucial opportunity due to situations out of our control?
- What if we hadn't worked 80-hour weeks for three years just to survive?
- What if closing those stores hadn't drained our savings and limited our ability to grow beyond one store that was left?

There are so many mixed feelings left from the Snack Lab experience. We succeeded in so many of our goals for this business yet were left with debt and questions after it was finished. How we see this incredible sequence of events during Snack Lab depends on your perspective:

Two Choices

When reflecting on the Snack Lab experience, I see two paths:

1. I could dwell on the misfortune of opening new stores just before the worst pandemic in a century. **Or**

2. I could choose gratitude—thankful that God gave us the privilege of creating something that touched and improved so many lives.

    I choose gratitude.

Snack Lab wasn't just a business; it was a mission. We were guided by a shared purpose: to bring nutritious, healthy food to our community and enrich the lives of people in Arkansas. Every decision, whether it succeeded or faltered, was made with that goal in mind.

Letting Go of "What-Ifs"

As I look back on this journey, I see God's hand in every step. While there are scars left by the challenges, they serve as reminders of His provision and grace. I no longer dwell on "what-ifs" or "if-onlys." Instead, I hold onto the blessings of the past nine years: the lessons learned, the lives impacted, and the partnership I shared with Emily.

Biblically, we're reminded in **Romans 8:28** that "all things work together for good to those who love God, to those who are called according to His purpose." Snack Lab wasn't just about food—it was about faith, resilience, and the universal truth that even in hardship, God works to reveal His greater plan.

I carry these lessons forward, with hope for what lies ahead.

Things I Should Regret, But Ended Up Being Blessings in Disguise

1. Moving to Oklahoma Chasing a Dream

For 13 years, I worked in the grocery business. My company, Phillips/Food 4 Less, was purchased by Walmart in 1992 as the retail giant entered the grocery market. We helped establish the first Supercenters—a fascinating experience. Yet, my ambition was to run a company, and that dream seemed unattainable at Walmart. While Walmart treated me well, I yearned for something different.

After fervent prayer, I made the decision to move my family to Oklahoma City to become president of a chain of 16 grocery stores. It was a bold step of faith. Within a year, the business thrived, but the owner chose to sell it. By God's grace, we hadn't yet sold the house we had built in Arkansas, even though we endured 10 months of paying two mortgages. Ultimately, we returned to Arkansas and were glad to be "home".

What could have been a regret became a moment of learning. I achieved my goal of running a business, and my family's support during that time was inspiring. This experience gave my children the confidence to pursue their own dreams fearlessly, even venturing across the country for college. We all grew stronger through that chapter of our lives.

2. Twenty Years in the Insurance Business

Insurance was never my passion, but it allowed me to focus on my family. The grocery business demanded 70-75 hours a week, which left little time for my kids. Stepping away from that world was a drastic life change, I don't regret it. It enabled me to coach my children in every sport, attend their school events, and be present for their milestones.

Beyond that, I discovered a love for coaching. For 18 years, even after my kids were grown, I coached 6th and 7th-grade football, as well as Baseball, softball, and basketball. Sometimes, taking a step back in one area of life allows you to leap forward in another. Those years were a gift I wouldn't trade for anything.

3. Jumping Into Snack Lab

Once again, I chased a dream—this time by co-founding Snack Lab. In the end, it cost us a lot of hard-earned savings and contributed to my deteriorating health, but as I look at it, I am very proud of what Emily and I built.

Snack Lab wasn't just a business; it was a way to help others lead healthier lives. While I definitely won't miss the 2:30 a.m. wake-up calls, I will never regret the journey.

4. High School and College Antics

Like many, I had my fair share of youthful misadventures. Who doesn't have those stories, right? Growing up in a small town, I had some wild moments: reckless driving, beer-drinking escapades, and questionable choices with friends in my well known Jeep. The local police knew me well enough that they would just stop me to confiscate my beer.

While my parents likely regretted those years, I don't. Those experiences taught me about boundaries and consequences. More importantly, they forged lifelong friendships and shaped the person I am today. By God's grace, I survived those reckless days and emerged with invaluable lessons.

5. Eating Like It Was My Last Meal

For 52 years, I approached every meal like it was my last. The first 25 years were understandable—as a kid playing sports and constantly on the move at 100 mph, I ate anything in sight. But the next 27 years had no excuse. My eating habits led to obesity and health challenges. Yet, even in this regret, I find blessings…

As a health coach, I've walked the same path as my clients. My own struggles give me empathy and insight, enabling me to guide others effectively. God's strength is made perfect in our weaknesses (2 Corinthians 12:9), and my journey with food is a testament to His redemptive power.

6. Red-Headed, Freckled-Faced, and Sunburned

Every Thursday (my dad was usually off on Thursdays) and Sunday, my family spent at the lake, water skiing from dawn until dusk. Winters were reserved for bird hunting. Back in the 1960s, sunblock wasn't a thing—only

Coppertone suntan oil, which was more like frying oil for our skin. You could literally hear your skin sizzle in the hot sun!

Years of lawn mowing jobs and outdoor jobs shirtless added to the damage. The result? A lifetime of skin problems, including melanomas and carcinomas. Yet, I wouldn't trade those sunburns for the memories. The sunburns were a result of a childhood full of memories that made me who I am today, and I loved every minute of it!

7. Football Gets in Your Blood

Football was my passion, even after major knee surgeries—one in 7th grade and more in college. I wasn't the best player and I never thought I was, but I loved the game and the lessons it taught me about teamwork and perseverance.

Today, my knees remind me of those days every time I get out of bed. But despite the pain, I wouldn't change a thing. Football instilled values of resilience and camaraderie that have stayed with me for life. The sacrifice was worth the gain.

8. "Send Her Home!"

When my daughter Anna was eight, I started a traveling fast-pitch softball team called the Cobras. Coaching that team was one of the best experiences of my life. However, one decision still lingers in my memory.

It was the bottom of the 7th inning of the Arkansas State Championship, we were trailing 3-2 with one out and runners on 1st and 2nd. The next batter hit a single to left field. As the third-base coach, I was usually aggressive, but I held Taylor Young at third base, trusting the next batter to bring her home. Unfortunately, the next two batters struck out, and we lost. These girls had worked so hard, and they deserved better than that from me.

I regretted that decision at the time, feeling I had let the team down. But in hindsight, it became a turning point for us. The Cobras went on to win three State Championships, a Southwest Regional Championship, and even placed 2nd at Nationals one year. These girls were very special, and I will treasure the time with all of them. No regrets. COBRAS STRIKE- sssss!

9. Visiting One Last Time

Don Bingham was one of my closest friends growing up. From childhood mischief to being teammates in high school football and baseball, we shared countless memories. We parted ways temporarily for college but later landed in Fayetteville at The University of Arkansas. We also worked at Sirloin Stockade in Springdale and ended up co-managing the restaurant for a while. One thing that always stayed with me about Don was that he was adamant on keeping in touch and was consistent with it, something I learned from him.

At 42, Don was diagnosed with aggressive brain cancer. He fought valiantly, but we all knew time was short. I visited him a few times during his battle, but I missed the final opportunity to see him. I had planned a trip but canceled at the last minute, not realizing it would be my last chance. Don passed away shortly after.

I will always regret not seeing Don one last time. But his life taught me an invaluable lesson: never delay the opportunity to show love and support to those who matter most. I carry his memory with me and strive to honor it by prioritizing relationships and cherishing every moment.

Looking back, these experiences could have been regrets but instead, they became blessings, shaping my faith, my character, and my relationships. Each chapter of life, no matter how challenging, has been a testimony to God's grace and a reminder of His plans for our growth (Jeremiah 29:11).

Chapter 2 Food for Thought

1. Can you name 3 things or actions in your life that you regret?

A. ______________________________

____

____

B. ______________________________

____

____

C. ______________________________

____

____

2. **<u>Chapter 2 Challenge</u>**: Now take those 3 regrets and see if you can name some blessings in the long run that occurred because of those actions:

A. ______________________________

____

B. ______________________________

____

C. ______________________________

____

3. Describe your thoughts to the following Bible verse:

2 Corinthians 7:10

"For the sorrow that is according to the will of God produces a repentance without regret, leading to salvation, but the sorrow of the world produces death."

____

____

____

____

____

____

Chapter 3
The Eyes Have It

I am not one of those older people who sit around and lament, "The world is going to the dogs."

As we age, it's easy to fall into the trap of believing we are better than the next generation. While I don't think that's true, there are areas where society as a whole—not just the younger generation—has degenerated over the years. Two key aspects stand out:

1. Manners

2. Work Ethic

I'll discuss work ethic later, but for now, let's focus on manners.

What Are Manners?

By definition manners are:

- A way in which a thing is done or happens.
- A way of behaving toward others, especially in a socially correct manner that demonstrates respect.

Over the last nine years, we've interviewed hundreds of young people at Snack Lab—mostly teenagers but also those from diverse walks of life. The lack of manners, often tied to a lack of respect, has been striking. Here are some examples:

- Simple courtesies like saying "please" and "thank you" are becoming rare. It's not entirely gone, but the trend is worrying.

- Expressions like "yes, sir" or "no, ma'am" are fading. Personally, I still say "ma'am" to everyone, regardless of age—and trust me, most people are younger than me!

- A firm handshake paired with eye contact is almost extinct. Today, there is a lot of wimpy, half-hearted hand-grazing. Years ago, as a grocery buyer, I wouldn't trust a sales rep who couldn't give me a confident handshake and look me in the eye. To me, it signaled trustworthiness.

- Basic acts of kindness, like holding the door open for others or letting a car merge into traffic, seem to have been lost in the rush of modern life.
- Public profanity has become normalized. While I understand the world evolves, there's no excuse for using offensive language in public. If you need to vent, keep it under your breath.

Life Lesson #3: Look People in the Eye

One of the simplest but most effective ways to connect with others is through eye contact.

A Challenge for You:

This week, as you walk down a busy street, look each person in the eye and say, "Good morning" or "hello." The responses might surprise you. Beware of some crazy reactions. Some will avoid your gaze, thinking you're either a serial killer or up to no good. Others, however, may smile and respond, perhaps reminded that we were created by God to connect with one another.

In today's fast-paced world, genuine human interaction is rapidly eroding. Technology—be it TVs, cell phones, or social media—has taken precedence over face-to-face relationships. It really baffles my mind to see people crossing busy intersections with their eyes glued to their phones or teenagers sitting together but engaging only through their screens.

At Snack Lab, we made it a strict policy: if someone interviewing for a job didn't make eye contact, they were not hired. Why? Because part of being a "Snack Barista" is understanding and relating to guests and being their trusted advisor about the type of food they should consume. It's impossible to do that without truly seeing them.

"Character is a quality that embodies many important traits, such as integrity, courage, perseverance, confidence, wisdom, and good manners. Unlike your fingerprints, which you are born with and cannot change, character is something you create within yourself and must take responsibility for **changing**.*"*

– Jim Rohn

Jim Rohn's words reflect the true reality of today's world. Manners and respect are integral parts of building character, and as parents, it's our God-given responsibility to teach these virtues to our children.

Parents, listen closely:

- It is your sacred duty to instill respect in your children.
- Teach them good manners and emulate those manners in your daily life.

The foundation for these lessons must be laid early. If you don't demonstrate and live out acts of kindness and respect before your children turn twelve, the chances of them adopting these virtues might be hopelessly low. My parents taught me the basic manners or communication and respect at an early age!

I want to be the kind of person my dog thinks I am

Have you ever thought about the resolute loyalty and love of dogs? They don't judge or hold grudges; they simply trust and forgive. They remind us of the kind of people we aspire to be.

Ellie, our yellow lab who passed away several years ago, embodied these qualities. She spent her days waiting patiently for us, cherishing every tiny moment we shared—whether it was swimming, walking, or splitting an apple in the evenings—she loved them. Her loyalty and forgiveness never flinched, even when we fell short of her expectations.

In many ways, I want to be the person my dog thought I was. I strive to be loyal to my family and friends, forgiving of others' faults, and able to see the good in everyone.

As humans, we will falter. We'll prioritize ourselves too much or fail to treat others as we should. But what matters most is the daily effort to improve—to treat others with kindness, patience, and respect.

Let us reflect on the love and loyalty our dogs show us and use it as inspiration to better ourselves. Each day is a new opportunity to grow, to connect with others, and to be the kind of person who reflects God's love in the way we live.

Chapter 3 Food for Thought

1. I challenged you earlier in this chapter to walk down the street, look people in the eye, smile and say "Good Morning" or "Hello" to strangers walking toward you or standing with you at a street corner.

   Write down the results of your experiment. What was their response?

   ____

   ____

   ____

   ____

   How did it make you feel?

   ____

   ____

   ____

   ____

   What are your plans going forward about addressing people to their face and looking them in the eye? Has your opinion changed?

____

____

____

____

2. What manners are you or your children currently lacking
   and what is your plan to improve that area in your life:

____

____

____

____

3. **<u>Chapter 3 Challenge</u>**:

*As a family, come up with a goal (or series of goals) for you
as a family to show more respect for others and your
family members:*

____

____

____

Chapter 4
How Do I Fix It?

It was more than just an eye-opening experience. Let's rewind a bit for some context…

As a kid, my parents used to say, "If you want to grow up big and strong, you need to eat lots of meat and potatoes and drink plenty of milk." Back in the 60s, that's what everyone believed. I took them at their word. I ate all the meat and potatoes I could get my hands on and drank over a gallon of milk every single day. That's no exaggeration—we had 8 half-gallons of milk delivered twice a week!

We always had a head of beef in the freezer, so it wasn't unusual for me to have steak and potatoes twice a day. Later, I went to college on a football scholarship. The athletes had access to an all-you-can-eat chow line, which, of course, included steak and potatoes. And let me tell you, the cold, crisp milk from those refrigerated containers was like a dream come true.

I carried my eating habits from childhood into college, but the difference was I worked out three to four hours a day. Back then, it didn't matter what I ate—it all turned into muscle. But when I stopped playing football, my workouts decreased drastically while my eating habits stayed the same.

In grad school, I worked at a steakhouse and took full advantage of the employee perks. All-you-can-eat steak and potatoes remained my go-to, but now Coke (or "soft drinks," as it's called elsewhere) replaced milk as my drink of choice. For the next 30 years, I kept up this diet, and by the time I reached my 50s, my body was paying the price.

At my heaviest, I weighed 390 pounds. I was a full insulin-dependent diabetic, and I'd developed high blood pressure, high cholesterol, sleep apnea, and neuropathy.

I was taking nine pills a day, poking myself with insulin shots twice daily, and barely had the energy to make it through the day. My doctors didn't mince words: it wasn't a matter of *if* I'd have a heart attack but *when.*

I was at rock bottom, completely overwhelmed and unsure of what to do. I'll never forget how humiliating it was to live life as such a large person:

- **The Post Office Scale:** The most embarrassing moment was realizing I had to go to the post office to weigh myself because the scales at my doctor's office didn't go that high.
- **Flying:** Flying was a nightmare. I still remember the looks on passengers' faces as I walked down the aisle. They didn't say anything, but their expressions screamed, *Please don't sit next to me!*
- **The Seatbelt Extension:** Once, after I squeezed into a seat, the flight attendant loudly handed me a seatbelt extender, announcing, "Here you go, sir. It looks like you'll need this."
- **Public Embarrassment:** My kids never said anything, but their faces sometimes revealed their embarrassment at my size.

- **Restaurant Booths:** I couldn't sit in a booth at some restaurants—it was physically impossible.

I'm not looking for sympathy. I knew these moments were my own doing, and I knew I had to change. That said, these experiences taught me something valuable: I now have deep empathy for others who are struggling with their weight. Society can be brutally unkind, and those moments, however painful, shaped the way I see the world today.

Don't get me wrong—I tried every diet known to man over that 30-year period. I lost weight on most of them for a few weeks, only to slip back into self-destructive patterns and gain it all back—plus more. Lose 20 pounds, gain back 30. Lose 40, gain back 50. I tried them all: the South Beach Diet, Richard Simmons' "Deal-a-Meal," the Grapefruit Diet, the Low-Fat Diet, the low-sugar diet, and my absolute favorite—the Atkins Diet. That was my dream diet: eat all the meat and cheese you could pile onto a plate, and the weight would supposedly melt away. I stuck with it long enough to lose 35 pounds—and gain back 55, along with 100 points on my cholesterol!

Before   **After**

As always, I carried on with life as if nothing had happened. I worked hard at my job, spent all my spare time with my kids and family, and ignored my health. After all, if you don't act like there's a problem, it will go away…right?

It didn't. I was struggling with disease, and I tried to justify it with every excuse I could think of:

- "I'm just destined to be overweight—it's in my genes."
- "My parents always said I was just 'big-boned.'"
- "I'll lose some weight next month."
- "If I keep taking these medications, I'll be fine."
- "Nothing can help this disease, so why bother trying?"

When I was first diagnosed with diabetes (I already had a slew of other self-inflicted health issues by then), I was sent to a class at Mercy Hospital meant to teach patients how to manage the condition. The nurse running the class opened with a grim statement:

"You have now been diagnosed with diabetes, a disease that will progressively worsen over time. There is no cure, and you will likely lose a limb, your eyesight, or more. One day, it will likely be the cause of your death."

I don't know about you, but just reading that statement is depressing. When I got home, I told Debbie that I felt hopeless. Later, I discovered that the nurse's information wasn't entirely accurate. There is light at the end of the tunnel—if you're willing to do the work. I had simply been looking in the wrong places.

This was in 1998. I managed to "live" with my conditions through medication: nine pills a day, two insulin shots daily, and a CPAP machine to keep me breathing at night. I did my best to lose weight, but nothing ever worked permanently. Eventually, I learned that one of the diabetes medications I was taking actually caused weight gain! Imagine that—taking medication because you're overweight, only for it to make you gain more weight. It's an endless cycle of frustration.

I kept going, though. Life didn't stop for my struggles, and neither did I. But something had to change.

Fast forward twelve years after starting this process, and I was still in poor health. My weight fluctuated between 340 and 390 pounds, and my medical conditions continued to worsen. In October 2010, Debbie and I visited her father at the nursing home. He had suffered a heart attack and stroke, leading to the final thirteen years of his life in that facility. While Debbie tended to her father, I encountered a woman in the neighboring room. She was 53 years old— my age at the time—and had recently lost both her legs to diabetes. She spoke of her despair and hopelessness. We prayed together, and I offered words of comfort.

Yet, as I listened to her, my thoughts began to drift. All I could envision was myself in her position, confined to a bed, legless and overwhelmed. The image consumed me. That night, I returned home filled with anguish and shed many tears. I prayed fervently, asking God to show me a way to overcome my negligence regarding my health. While my prayers should have been focused on the woman I met,

I found myself consumed by one question: "What am I going to do?"

As He always does, God answered me—the same answer He had placed in my heart countless times before, though I had been unwilling to hear it. My health, like every other part of my life, needed to serve God. Despite being a Christian since I was 22 years old, I had compartmentalized my faith, excluding my health from God's guidance. I relied on willpower and grit to address my health, but it was futile. Through prayer, I finally surrendered and allowed God to lead me.

Life Lesson #4: If you want to change something in your life, start by changing your heart.

Romans 12:2: "Don't copy the behavior and customs of this world, but let God transform you into a new person by changing the way you think."

Matthew 19:26: "Jesus looked at them and said, 'With man this is impossible, but with God all things are possible.'"

What I've learned is this: true, lasting change doesn't come from the head or willpower alone. It begins in the heart—as a gift from God. The world tells us we can handle everything on our own. Our minds insist, "You can do this." But the truth is, nothing meaningful happens without God's hand guiding us.

So, what did I do? I prayed, consulted with several doctors, and prayed some more. I realized I needed a spark to initiate a new lifestyle, but I wanted a long-term solution, not a quick fix. I decided to undergo weight-loss surgery, not as a cure but as a fresh start.

Anyone who thinks weight-loss surgery is the easy way out hasn't experienced it. The first three months post-surgery demand strict adherence to dietary rules, and any deviation results in immediate physical consequences. I've seen many people revert to old habits within a few months of surgery, proving that the procedure itself isn't the answer. Success depends on a transformed heart and a commitment to a new way of living.

For me, the surgery marked a turning point. If I could thrive by eating only what my body allowed during those early months, why not continue that lifestyle indefinitely?

I resolved to eat only real food—nothing from a box, pouch, can, or bag. I didn't have to read labels, count calories, count macros, or any of those self-defeating methods. By eating slowly and listening to my body, I learned to stop when I was satisfied and to eat only when I was truly hungry.

I quickly discovered two important truths:

1.   Our bodies need far less food than our minds believe.
2.   What foods we eat matters as much as the quantity.

We have to keep learning:

The main difference between school and life: In school, you're taught a lesson and then given a test.   In life, you're given a test that teaches you a lesson.

How often do we wish we could convey our hard-earned wisdom to younger generations? If only they truly grasped how their choices now would shape their future. Yet, we were no different in our youth. Back then, I thought I knew everything. Now, the older I get, the more I realize how little I truly know. At this rate, I can't afford to grow much older!

Never stop learning. The day you cease to learn is the day you truly stop living.

The other half of the equation was exercise. In college, I worked out extensively while playing football, but as my career and family responsibilities grew, exercise teetered off a lot and ultimately became a distant memory. I told myself there wasn't enough time. Over the years, I joined every gym in Northwest Arkansas but rarely used them. I tried walking and running, but at 390 pounds with bad knees, the pain outweighed the benefits.

When I began my weight-loss journey, I set a goal: once I lost 50 pounds, I would reward myself with an elliptical machine. The first 50 pounds came off quickly, so I kept my promise and purchased a high-quality elliptical. This time, I actually used it!

Every evening, I spent at least 90 minutes on the machine. Exercise became something I craved rather than dreaded. Over time, as I lost more weight, I transitioned to outdoor activities, rediscovering my love for walking and being in nature. This simple change transformed my approach to physical activity.

By embracing a heart-centered approach to health—one rooted in faith and guided by God—I found a path to lasting change. My journey taught me the importance of aligning every aspect of my life with God's purpose. Through prayer, perseverance, and a willingness to learn, I began to reclaim my health and my life.

Every Day Is A Chance To Grow

Every day you wake up is a clean slate—an opportunity to become the person you aspire to be. Each morning offers a chance to make a change; all you have to do is decide to take it.

Too often, we waste energy beating ourselves up on yesterday's mistakes, forgetting the potential of today. Fools cling to the past, dreamers live in the future, but the present belongs to those who choose to act—today!

This lifestyle transformation lasted two years, during which I lost over 200 pounds. At my lowest, I weighed 188 pounds—a weight that felt too light for me. For the first time in my life, I set a goal to gain 20-25 pounds. Having worked so hard to lose weight, I was determined not to jeopardize my progress. Building muscle seemed the healthiest way to achieve my goal. Over the next year, I joined a gym called GPP and focused on strength training. This approach worked, and I added muscle to my once frail body.

Fourteen years later, I'm proud and grateful to have maintained my weight between 210 and 225 pounds.

While the physical changes were all great, the blessings that came during this time were even more profound:

1. Over the course of two years, I overcame high blood pressure, high cholesterol, sleep apnea, and even diabetes. Today, I'm proud to say that I haven't needed prescription medication in 12 years. This hard work has been a blessing, setting an example for my children and giving me the precious opportunity to be present in my grandchildren's lives. Thanks be to God!

2. Witnessing these changes in my health, I felt God guiding me to help others. A friend from GPP, Danielle Many, and I independently decided to become certified health coaches. We supported each other throughout the 10-month certification process, gaining invaluable knowledge together. Danielle went on to establish a successful endurance team, becoming a leader and

role model for many. I am immensely proud of her achievements.

As for me, I also embraced the role of a health coach, guiding others toward healthier lifestyles. This journey led to the creation of Snack Lab, a project I co-founded with Emily Amadon. Over the past nine years, Snack Lab has touched countless lives across Northwest Arkansas. I am forever grateful to God for leading me down this path. You never know where He will guide you—just listen and follow your heart.

We all struggle with aspects of our lives that need change. The world often leads us down destructive paths we can't fully understand. My advice to you, regardless of your age or circumstances, is this: stop fighting against the current. Let God come to you. You will never regret it.

Don't Let The World Dictate Your Definition Of Success

When asked, "What do you do?" have you ever heard a mother respond, "I'm just a stay-at-home mom"? *Just*? The most important job in the world has been relegated to "just" a stay-at-home mom. Mothers should never feel the need to apologize for the incredible impact they have on their children's lives.

Money, power, and possessions are terrible ways to keep score! Where you work, what is your "title" or how much money you make are poor measures of success. They don't define your worth. True success lies in what brings you joy and how you positively impact others.

Let your life reflect the beauty of the unique gifts you've been given. Don't let the world convince you that you are "just" anything.

Chapter 4 Food for Thought

1. Can you think of a few things in your life you need to change? List anything you truly want to change:

A. ____

____

____

B. ____

____

____

C. ____

____

____

2. Now look at the list of things above that you want to change. Ask yourself for each one of them- is this just for me and my selfish needs, or is it something that will serve God and other people? Weed the list down to only the changes that will serve God and other people:

____

____

____

3. What excuses have you made throughout your life why you didn't make these changes?

A. _______________________________________

____

____

B. _______________________________________

____

____

____

C. _______________________________________

____

____

4. **<u>Chapter 4 Challenge</u>**: Set aside an hour of one day this week for prayer about this change in your life. Pray, but more than anything else, listen to God and what he is telling you. Write down what you have learned from this exercise.

____

____

____

____

Chapter 5
The Best Ability

I previously mentioned that two key characteristics that seem to have eroded in society are good manners and work ethic. While we've already discussed good manners and will revisit them later, I now want to address a vital component of work ethic: showing up. Legendary NFL coach Bill Parcells once said, "The best ability is availability," and he couldn't be more right. This principle holds true not only in sports but in every aspect of life:

1. Showing up at work every day, ready to do whatever the job entails.

2. Showing up for your kids, being there when they need you—a responsibility that never truly ends.

3.   Showing up for your spouse, supporting them through life's challenges.

4.   Showing up for your parents, no matter what or when they need your help.

5.   Being available for friends in need, and even for strangers when the opportunity arises.

6.   Taking accountability for your actions, especially when you've made mistakes or hurt others.

7.   Showing up for God through prayer, study, and acts of service.

Integrity is a word often thrown around a lot in conversations but not always fully understood. At its core, integrity means being reliable—someone who can be counted on to show up when they say they will. Can people depend on you?

Life Lesson #5: Show Up

Having been in business leadership roles for over 45 years, I've seen every excuse imaginable for not showing up to work. Some are legitimate, but many are not. Here are a few of the more colorful excuses I've encountered:

- "My grandmother is on her deathbed." Strangely, it's never just that she's not well. As a matter of fact, an employee claimed this three separate times—prompting me to ask how she could possibly have three grandmothers!
- "I have a doctor's appointment this morning and won't be able to come in all day." How long does a doctor's appointment last, anyway?
- "My car won't start." Ever heard of Uber?
- "I need to take my dog to the vet."

Experience has shown me that more than half of sick calls happen on Mondays. Coincidence? Perhaps, but I suspect not!

"Be a warrior when it comes to delivering on your ambitions and dreams and a saint when it comes to treating people with respect, modeling generosity, and showing up with outright love." — Robin S. Sharma

Showing Up With Purpose

While it's important to physically be where you're supposed to be, showing up also means being mentally and emotionally present and approaching the task with a positive attitude.

One of my most rewarding experiences was coaching youth football for 18 years, primarily working with 6th and 7th graders. One of my sideline jobs that I absolutely loved! It was a privilege to watch these young boys develop not just their football skills but their character and maturity. Joey was one of the most memorable players I coached, and his story is a testament to the power of showing up with the right attitude.

Joey joined my team as a 6th grader, though he looked like a 3rd grader. He weighed no more than 65 pounds and was probably shorter than I was in first grade. Yet Joey had something special—a fire in his eyes. He looked me straight in the eye, listened attentively, and always responded with "yes, sir" or "no, sir." His father told me how proud Joey was of his football uniform and pads, and that was all I needed to know.

I had a rule for all first-year players: everyone had to play on the offensive line. I loved playing that position myself and believed it offers great training for not only football, but generally in life. Offensive line is the only position in any sport where you play your entire career with your back to the ball. It is truly not about you- it's about the team. Your whole goal is to help someone on your team succeed, and the only time you will ever hear your number called is when you get a.penalty It's not about personal glory; it's all about the team.   Joey embraced this philosophy wholeheartedly.

Despite his small size, Joey gave 100% on every play. He pushed, fought, and gave his all, even when it seemed like he was barely making an impact. Yet his spirit and determination inspired everyone, including me. By the end of the season, Joey had become my best offensive lineman.

The following year, Joey had grown to about 75 pounds, and I moved him to linebacker as a reward for his hard work. However, after a few practices, Joey approached me with a surprising request: "Coach, would you mind if I played on the offensive line again? I've been practicing against your linemen, and they need the help."

His selflessness brought tears to my eyes. Joey understood that life isn't about personal gain but about contributing wherever you're needed. I explained to Joey that while his willingness to sacrifice for the team was admirable, my job as a coach was also to look out for his growth. "Joey," I said, "just like you want to do what's best for the team, I need to do what's best for you. As you get older, you may not be big enough to play on the line, but your attitude and drive make you a natural leader. I need your leadership as a linebacker this year. You can be a great football player and an even better person if you keep that attitude."

Joey thrived as a linebacker, leading our team to a league championship that year. He continued to play linebacker through junior high and high school.. Though he wasn't big enough to play in college, Joey was an All-American in my eyes. He always showed up for his team, and that mindset carried over into his adult life. Today, Joey is a college graduate with a wonderful family, and I have no doubt he shows up for them every single day.

Failure is not the opposite of success; it's a part of success!

Abraham Lincoln once said, "My greatest concern is not whether you have failed, but whether you are content with your failure."

Many people spend their entire life afraid to chase their dreams, because of their apprehensions. "what if this happens, or that happens" and I fail? These shackles of self-doubt never allow them to explore their dreams and witness if they might have made it.

The key to achieving important goals and dreams is unwavering persistence and a belief in yourself. It is about showing up every day without the fear in heart that you might fail and never quitting. If we do that, the results will take care of themselves. I have had many goals and dreams in my life; some I could achieved, and some I didn't quite get there.

After chasing dreams all my life, turning some into success while failing miserably at some, here's the thing I understood:

I gained as much from the goals and dreams I didn't achieve as I did from the ones I made!

You see, it's in pushing forward through the fear and showing up that's makes us truly unbeatable!

Do you want to change your life? Don't let fear of failure hold you back, because pushing through the fear is the true victory! If you want to improve any phase of your health, whether it is physical, mental, emotional, or spiritual health, go for it! There's nothing to lose, and EVERYTHING to gain!

****

Sometimes the hardest thing to do is to show up for yourself. As I told you, I worked out a lot when I was playing sports. For example, in the Summers before Football practices started in High School and in College, I would push myself work out every day. I worked for Ozark Fence Company during the day, usually digging post holes or carrying wire. At lunches, I would go to the football fields and do the running for the day- usually 100's, 200's, or longer distances. I went back and built fence until 5:00 and either played a baseball game in American Legion or went to the pool and swam. I also lifted weights 3-4 times per week. When I look back on that, what made me do it each day? I was driven to work that hard because the competition drove me. I knew other people were working hard as well.

As I got out of sports and got into the hustle bustle of life, I couldn't find the motivation to show up every day and workout. I did everything I could to make exercise a part of my routine, but it always seemed to fizzle out. When my life and health changed for the better, a big part of it was consistent exercise EVERY DAY. Why did it work this time when it had failed miserably the last 30 years? The answer is simple- I was showing up for myself! I finally realized that I can't serve others unless I am taking care of myself as well. I realized my health was worth it, and you know what- I began to look forward to exercising. No longer was it something I dreaded; it was kind of my treat for the day. When it becomes a part of who you are, you miss it when you aren't able to do it consistently.

I have learned a lot of important lessons in my life, but showing up may be the most important one of all. Showing up is a simple concept, yet it's tied inexorably to our character and beliefs. You see, showing up in the long run is about caring for something more than just yourself. And when that happens, it really does become a simple concept.

John 10:10

"The thief comes only to steal and kill and destroy. I came that they may have life and have it abundantly."

Chapter 5 Food for Thought

1. What are some of the things you "show up" for every day:

A____

____

____

B____

____

____

C____

____

____

3. What are some things you count on others to show up for in your life:

A. ____

____

____

B. ____

____

- **<u>Chapter 5 Challenge</u>**: Pick one thing you believe you can do a better job of showing up for, and write a short game plan for achieving that objective:

____

____

____

____

____

- Read the bible verse on the previous page from John 10:10. What does it mean to you?

____

____

____

____

Chapter 6
Tell Me Your Story

As I worked with God to heal my disease through proper nutrition, I began to realize that living a healthy lifestyle is more than just a slogan. The human body, designed by God, is undoubtedly the most perfect piece of equipment ever created. It's a delicate balance of energy and action, functioning in ways that are impossible for us to fully grasp. Yet, there's one flaw in this perfect design—*us*. If we will just get out of the way and eat as God intended, our body will continue to function properly. It's humans who disrupt this natural balance that God designed by continuing to put processed, man-made products full of artificial sweeteners, excessive salt, and unhealthy fats.

As I grew in this understanding, I felt compelled to share my insights with others. I wanted—*needed*—to help people see the potential for transformation when we follow God's plan for our health. I researched and discovered an excellent program that offered certification as an Integrative Health Coach. The process, which took about 10–11 months, was both energizing and uplifting. After earning my certification, I began working with clients to help them embrace healthier lifestyles.

A key principle I learned through my training was **bio-individuality**—the idea that everyone is unique.

To truly connect with people and address their needs, I had to meet them where they were and consider their individual circumstances.

To do this, I developed a "Lifestyle Analysis," a 45–60-minute session designed to explore the fundamental patterns of their lives:

- Family life and its triggers
- Work life and its challenges
- Family history—parents, childhood experiences, etc.
- Sleep habits—both quantity and quality
- Eating patterns
- Current exercise routines
- What makes them happy or sad
- Other frustrations

The things I realized from these sessions were astonishing yet logical. People's health, eating habits, and overall happiness are deeply intertwined. How someone eats is directly connected to their emotional fulfillment, personal satisfaction, and the well-being of those around them. All aspects of life, not just the food they consume, ultimately contribute to their overall health.

Most of the people I work with struggle with some area of their health—whether it's weight issues, chronic disease, or persistent pain. Their frustration is palpable. Almost without fail, during the Lifestyle Analysis, we touch on a pain point that brings them to tears. Whether the pain is at the surface or buried deep in their subconscious, it's often tied to their health challenges.

As I dug deeper into this work, I realized I needed additional training to address not just health issues but life challenges as well. I pursued certification as a Life Coach, equipping myself to help clients confront the emotional and mental barriers impeding their health.

What I learned was simple yet added great value:

1. Ask open-ended questions like, "Tell me your story about growing up," "What's your current family life like?" "What has your career been like?" or "What do you love to do?"

2. Avoid judgment. People can sense judgment, and it shuts down their willingness to open up. We all have stories to tell, but we need a safe space to share them without fear of being judged.

That second point has been a lifelong lesson for me. It's all too easy to judge others, isn't it? But I've learned, often the hard way, that **everybody has a story** to tell, and they want to tell it to someone that cares. To truly help someone, we must first empathize with their journey and understand how it shapes their life.

Life Lesson #6: Don't pre-judge people. Everyone has a story and challenges they've had to overcome.

"You don't teach morals and ethics and empathy and kindness in the schools. You teach that at home, and children learn by your example."
—Tarana Burke

"Finally, all of you, be like-minded, be sympathetic, love one another, be compassionate and humble."
—1 Peter 3:8

Understanding bio-individuality also means recognizing that life's experiences affect each of us differently. For example, our daughter Anna and her husband Ben have twins—a boy and a girl—who are just over two years old. These kids are an amazing testament to God's love, expressed uniquely in each of them.

Gabriel is thoughtful and reserved, always observing and processing the world around him. Genevieve, on the other hand, is the ringleader of a three-ring circus—chatty, animated, and eager to share whatever she's holding. They are raised in the same home, with the same parents, toys, and food, yet they respond to life in completely different ways. Watching their personalities unfold has been a joy. (By the way, as a grandfather, I highly recommend having twin grandkids—they are an absolute blast!)

This differentiation is a perfect example of bio-individuality. Just as food affects everyone differently, so do life's experiences.

As we grow, the way we handle adversity influences our overall health. Many of us struggle to forgive others for the pain they've caused, and perhaps even more, we struggle to forgive ourselves for our mistakes or failures. But learning to let go and heal is essential for true health—physically, emotionally, and spiritually.

FORGIVENESS

I have struggled, as I'm sure many of you have, to step free from the past, to move forward and not allow the weight of yesterday to consume my "now". A few nights ago, I heard a song, and the words ran through me like a lightning bolt. The song is "Bird Set Free" by Sia.   Here are some of the lyrics:

But there's a scream inside that we all try to hide.

We hold on so tight, we cannot deny.

Eats us alive, oh it eats us alive.

Yes, there's a scream inside that we all try to hide.

We hold on so tight, but I don't wanna die, no.

I'm not gonna care if I sing off key.

I find myself in my melodies.

I sing for love, I sing for me.

I shout it out like a bird set free.

This is Easter week, a time that reminds us of forgiveness and grace. Through the sacrifice of His son, God granted us immeasurable grace—a truth we commemorate today on Good Friday. If this is true, which I believe it is, then why do we struggle so to find the peace that God desires for us? Why do we persist in punishing ourselves for lessons we have already learned?

This week is about forgiveness, but that forgiveness must extend beyond others; it must reach inward. If I believe in the forgiveness God has offered, yet continue to wrestle with my past, the struggle lies within me, not with God. If I find no peace, if I remain trapped in the hole I dug for myself, perhaps the solution is to follow Christ's example and forgive myself. Only then can I move forward and become the person God sees me as already!

No matter what struggles weigh on your heart today, release them and forgive yourself. Follow the example Jesus gave us. Forgive yourself—God already has.

A couple of years ago, on Good Friday, I wrote the reflection above. I still believe it holds the key to our long-term well-being. Can we forgive those who have wronged us? Can we forgive ourselves for failing to understand others and their unique stories? Everyone carries a story, often more than one. Too often, we are so busy living *in* our lives that we forget to step back and reflect *on* them. True change may require us to first make peace with our past. This can be a daunting task, but it is essential.

LEARN TO LOVE YOUR SCARS

We all bear scars, don't we? Some are visible, etched on our skin, while others are hidden, buried deep in our memories without a single mark showing their existence. Over the years, I've come to appreciate scars of all kinds.

They signify that the hurt is over, the wound has closed and healed. Unless we choose to reopen them, scars are simply reminders of where we have been and what we have overcome.

I believe God allows these scars to remain as evidence of His healing power. Physical scars, like emotional ones, serve as markers of His grace. Though some scars never fully disappear, they stand as testaments to the depth of His love and the abundance of His mercy.

As time passes, the scars on my body have faded, and so have those on my heart. But like my physical scars, the emotional ones soften with each passing year. When we choose to move forward, these scars transform from reminders of pain to symbols of resilience and gratitude.

Are you ready to move past your scars? Are you willing to look ahead and create new memories? No matter what has happened in your past, you have the power to build a new life from this moment forward. God is healing your scars, rooting for you to embrace His grace and the blessings He bestows every day.

Judgment and a lack of empathy have fueled wars, murders, and hatred throughout history. Prejudice and animosity are often passed down through generations and perpetuated by societal influences, including modern media. Empathy, however, can be taught—at home, in classrooms, in Sunday schools, in churches, and beyond. It takes effort to understand others, but it is a worthwhile endeavor. Much of the divisiveness in today's political landscape stems from a failure to truly see and understand one another.

If there's one lesson I've learned in my 67 years, it's this: everyone has a story, and that story shapes who they are in countless ways. The art of listening is the key to understanding. My father once told me, "God gave you two ears and one mouth. If you listen twice as much as you talk, you might learn something."

Consider the wisdom of Romans 14:1-13:

1 Accept the one whose faith is weak, without quarreling over disputable matters.

2 One person's faith allows them to eat anything, but another, whose faith is weak, eats only vegetables.

3 The one who eats everything must not treat with contempt the one who does not, and the one who does not eat everything must not judge the one who does, for God has accepted them.

4 Who are you to judge someone else's servant? To their own master, servants stand or fall. And they will stand, for the Lord is able to make them stand.

5 One person considers one day more sacred than another; another considers every day alike. Each of them should be fully convinced in their own mind.

6 Whoever regards one day as special does so to the Lord. Whoever eats meat does so to the Lord, for they give thanks to God; and whoever abstains does so to the Lord and gives thanks to God.

7 For none of us lives for ourselves alone, and none of us dies for ourselves alone.

8 If we live, we live for the Lord; and if we die, we die for the Lord. So, whether we live or die, we belong to the Lord.

9 For this very reason, Christ died and returned to life so that he might be the Lord of both the dead and the living.

10 You, then, why do you judge your brother or sister? Or why do you treat them with contempt? For we will all stand before God's judgment seat.

11 It is written: "'As surely as I live,' says the Lord, 'every knee will bow before me; every tongue will acknowledge God.'"

12 So then, each of us will give an account of ourselves to God.

13 Therefore let us stop passing judgment on one another. Instead, make up your mind not to put any stumbling block or obstacle in the way of a brother or sister.

Chapter 6
Food for Thought

1. Talk a little of your current family- tell your story:

A____

____

____

B____

____

____

C____

____

____

2. Talk about your career- what are you proudest of in your
    career?

A____

____

____

B____

____

3. **<u>Chapter 6 Challenge</u>**: This week, sit down and really talk to someone you don't know that well- or maybe someone you could possibly help. Have them tell you "their story"- whatever that is. You will have to pick the right time and place- it won't be easy. Record your thoughts about what you discovered.

____

____

____

- Re-read 1 Peter 3:8 above. What specific thing can you change in your life regarding this passage?

____

____

____

____

____

Let us learn to listen, understand, and extend grace to one another. In doing so, we honor God and grow closer to the peace He desires for all of us.

Chapter 7
Food to Fuel Your Life

Co-written by Emily Amadon

Lessons learned from 9 years with Snack Lab

1 Peter 4:10

"Each of you should use whatever gift you have received to serve others, as faithful stewards of God's grace in its various forms."

I want to share a story about my favorite dog, Ellie—a yellow lab who brought boundless joy to our family. Ellie *loved* swimming and retrieving. During that season of life, we were fortunate to have a swimming pool in our backyard. Every day when I came home, Ellie and I would head straight to the pool for our "workout." While I swam laps, she often joined me, her energy and enthusiasm infectious.

The highlight of our routine was playing fetch. I would toss a floating stick into the pool, and Ellie would leap in without hesitation, retrieve the stick, and bring it back to me, her tail wagging furiously.

Watching her fervently jump into the water time after time, regardless of the temperature or her fatigue, I realized something: If we approached life with the same joy and determination as Ellie did with fetch, we'd be much happier. Even when she was nearly too tired to climb out of the pool, Ellie kept going—not because she had to, but because she loved it. For her, it was not a chore.

This is a lesson worth pondering. Life isn't always easy, but the secret lies in finding something you love. Working hard at something you hate feels like torture. But when you love what you do, even the hardest challenges become fulfilling.

I think we can learn a lot from dogs- loyalty, how to have fun, and pure love for life. I am not suggesting we go around licking people or peeing in the yard- that could lead to trouble! But we can certainly embrace their spirit: do what you love, and do it with all your heart.

Ellie's love for fetch mirrors my journey with Snack Lab. My business partner, Emily Amadon, and I experienced the most challenging years of our lives building Snack Lab, yet we loved it deeply. Like Ellie diving in for the stick, we faced obstacle after obstacle, determined to see our vision through and the difference we are making in the lives of so many people.

She and I together solved a lot of problems and created a business approach that had not been seen in Northwest Arkansas previously. During those nine years the world kept "throwing another floating stick" at us, and we kept jumping in and bringing it back!

We're breaking this chapter into phases, each reflecting the lessons and successes from our nine years with Snack Lab. These years were filled with relentless effort, problem-solving, and countless moments of perseverance. We often joked about "fetching the stick" daily, but each challenge brought us closer to fulfilling our mission of creating something meaningful.

The "Snack Lab Years"

As told by Emily Amadon

If you've ever nurtured a dream or idea, you know how exhilarating it is to witness and imagine the way it could thrive. But bringing that dream to life? That's where the real work begins.

Snack Lab is a part healthy restaurant, part healthy convenience store concept that Bobby and I created from scratch. Our mission was to offer healthy snacks and grab + go meals for everybody seeking a healthy and active lifestyle. Believe me, there wasnothing like it anywhere in Northwest Arkansas! In the nine years of our time with Snack Lab, we survived, thrived, threw in the towel, and started again— daily. In Bobby's words, we kept "fetching the stick."

In our nine years with Snack Lab, we faced triumphs and setbacks—sometimes within the same day. As Bobby says, we just kept "fetching the stick." Those years were grueling, but they were also filled with growth, grit, and purpose.

Bobby and I could fill volumes with stories from those days. We often would recount these stories to each other after a long day, when all the employees had gone home (or in the wee morning hours before they had arrived). It was our way of saying, *"look how far we've come, partner."* A few of these stories really stick out—ones that we would reflect on over and over. Ones that would prove to be pivotal moments for how our Snack Lab journey evolved.

****

One: Location, Location, Location

Our first big challenge was finding the right location. Early on, we learned that a restaurant in an old house near the Bentonville square was closing, and the building was up for sale. It was a charming spot, perfectly situated near biking trails and the heart of the community. We toured the property, envisioned its potential, and made an offer.

Within twenty-four hours, we received devastating news: we'd been outbid, and no counteroffers would be entertained. It felt like a crushing setback.

But hindsight reveals God's hand in moments like these. That disappointment was the first of many divine interventions that would guide Snack Lab's journey.

Not long after, we discovered a location a few miles south in a new development. The space allowed for a custom build-out, the price was reasonable, and—perhaps most importantly—we gained a landlord who proved to be a rare blessing: fair, collaborative, and open to ideas: a rare find. This partnership became instrumental to our success. In October 2016, we signed the lease for our first Snack Lab location, with construction set to begin that December.

Isaiah 41:10

"So do not fear, for I am with you; do not be dismayed, for I am your God. I will strengthen you and help you; I will uphold you with my righteous right hand."

Lesson learned:

The harder you try to MAKE things happen yourself, the more difficult it becomes.   Just trust in the process and God's Grace.

****

Two—Good Growth, Bad Growth

Snack Lab opened its doors for business in April 2017. We had spent several months promoting our concept before the launch, and this preparation laid a strong foundation. Customers showed up on our first days, and we quickly realized we had something special with our concept. Sales exceeded our projections within months, and within the first year, we expanded our kitchen and seating areas. This growth was a blessing and a testament to God's provision, as we found favor with a landlord willing to work with our needs. Our small but passionate kitchen crew created healthy food that burst with flavor. We were working crazy hard and having fun—this was our good growth.

Bobby and I tackled the many challenges of starting a small business from scratch. We frequently heard customers say, "I wish you'd open a store in [city name]," almost daily, if not hourly, sparking dreams of expanding to Fayetteville, Little Rock, or even Kansas City. However, with my first child on the way, we decided to keep any new location close to home. Balancing ambition with family was not easy, but we sought wisdom and prayerfully considered our next steps.

After months of discussions with landlords and developersin the area, we narrowed our options to two locations: Rogers and Fayetteville. We signed a lease for Rogers, aiming to open in late 2019, and soon after, another lease for Fayetteville, with a projected opening in March 2020. Little did we know the trials ahead.

Expanding to multiple locations introduced challenges that felt like an endless game of whack-a-mole. Staffing issues, operational constraints, slower-than-expected sales in the new locations, and management gaps began to surface. Then, as if to test our resolve further, guess what happened: a small thing called Covid- a global pandemic the likes of which changed everybody's life, hit the week we opened our Fayetteville location! It was a storm we were ill-prepared to weather, and the impact was devastating. The pandemic forced us to close our Rogers location, leaving us heartbroken but determined to press on.

Fayetteville endured for several more years, but the challenges continued. Operating across two counties and a 30-minute drive stretched our resources thin. Despite our belief in Fayetteville's potential, our finances and energy dwindled. We reached a painful crossroads: risk everything to sustain Fayetteville or focus solely on healing our

Bentonville store that was hemorrhaging from Covid as well. Exhausted in every way imaginable, we made the difficult decision to close Fayetteville and redirect our efforts toward Bentonville. Though weary, we felt God's gentle guidance to simplify and rebuild.

Lesson Learned: *Understand why your business is successful before pursuing growth. More isn't always better.*

Bonus Lesson Learned: *Closing a store with an ongoing lease is neither cheap nor easy.*

Three—The Secret Sauce

One of the greatest realizations during our journey of growth and retraction was that Bobby and I were integral to Snack Lab's "secret sauce." Expanding to multiple locations diluted our personal involvement, and with it, some of the magic that had made our concept thrive. But what is it about he and I that made magic happen?

As entrepreneurs, we knew no one would care for our business like we did. Snack Lab was an extension of us, and our commitment was evident in every detail. Bobby started his days at 3 a.m., and we both worked tirelessly to maintain our high standards. We saw the details and nuance of the business that no one else saw—the way we merchandised our products and sourced ingredients; the way we crafted our marketing messages; the way we talked to customers; the way we cared for catering and special orders. Even small details, like the placement of our famous Maple Granola, mattered deeply to us.

Bobby's talent for sales and merchandising complemented my focus on brand marketing and operations to a very high standard. We were customer service mavericks that anticipated customer needs, and often beat up on each other until the product or process came out just right.. Our passion raised the bar so high that it was difficult for others to replicate our efforts or match our level of dedication. This made scaling to multiple locations challenging, as we struggled to delegate the same care and precision.

Reflecting on this, I am reminded of Psalm 127:1: *"Unless the Lord builds the house, those who build it labor in vain."* In our case, Bobby and I were the builders, but the "house" was sustained by God's grace and our reliance on Him. Our experience taught us that success isn't merely about hard work—it's about stewardship, wisdom, and faith in the process.

We never stopped trying. We never stopped striving to improve and to disseminate our knowledge with our staff. Bobby and I both cared deeply that our customers received excellent care from everyone on our team. If a single bowl was missed in an order, we would deliver it ourselves. (During COVID, we delivered *everything*!) Rarely did we say no to special requests—even the most unusual ones, which could fill an entire book. I'll never forget making breakfast for 50 people during a snowstorm, delivering it myself so a movie production could continue filming. Thank goodness for four-wheel drive!

Ultimately, the magic of Snack Lab wasn't about Bobby or me. The true magic lay in how our customers felt seen and valued, and how they used our products to positively impact their lives. Bobby and I simply worked hard to ensure that happened as often as possible. Snack Lab was a place where we listened to people's unique dietary needs and made their requests a reality. We felt that our customers were guests in our home. They came to us with food sensitivities and special health goals, and we helped them find options they could safely eat and enjoy.

We heard stories of lives transformed—better lab results, renewed energy, weight loss, reduced dependence on medication, and overall improved well-being. On our hardest days, it always seemed a customer would reach out to Bobby or me just to say how much they appreciated what Snack Lab had done for them. Every time we "fetched the stick," we knew we were helping one more person in our community.

Lesson learned:

"If people like you, they'll listen to you. But if they trust you, they'll do business with you."

— Zig Ziglar

Four—The Ending is Never Easy

After returning to just one store, Bobby and I focused on "righting the ship"—restoring profitability and finding sustainable ways to grow sales without spreading ourselves too thin. We stopped working late into the evenings at home, which I know our spouses appreciated. We strengthened our core team and expanded our product offerings. We began to grow sales of our beloved granola through participation in a local farmer's market, expanding the line to include new granola flavors, trail mixes, and healthy cookies, and re-branded it as "Snack Lab Honest Snacks." These steps were good and necessary, yet we couldn't ignore the sense that our time at Snack Lab was drawing to a close.

As I type this, Spotify is playing a song that perfectly captures our journey: *Hard Fought Hallelujah* by Brandon Lake.

I'll bring my hard-fought, heartfelt

been-through-hell hallelujah *(ooh, ooh)*

And I'll bring my storm-tossed, torn-sail

story-to-tell hallelujah, oh.

'Cause God, *You've* been patient

God, *You've* been gracious

Faithful, whatever *I'm* feeling or facing.

Our journey with Snack Lab was filled with many challenges, but lots of "Hard-fought Hallelujahs" as well. When bank accounts were empty, resources appeared. When we were short on staff, help arrived. On days we doubted, a customer's kind words reminded us of our impact. These moments weren't just luck; they were *God moments*—hard-fought hallelujahs that strengthened our faith.

After nine years of building Snack Lab, a buyer approached us, and we knew it was time to let go. On October 1, 2024, we handed over control of the business we loved. No longer would we decide what products to sell, how the store would look, or whether it would succeed. Letting go was both hard and right—right for us, our families, and for giving Snack Lab the fresh ideas and leadership it needed.

Did we succeed? It depends on how you measure success. By traditional business standards, perhaps not. We struggled with inconsistent profits and sales growth and couldn't scale as we'd hoped, for many reasons. But by *our* standards, we were absolutely successful. We showed up every day, ready to fulfill what the Lord placed before us. We "fetched the stick" over and over, pouring love into our community. For us, that was the truest measure of success.

As Ecclesiastes 3:1 reminds us:

"There is a time for everything, and a season for every activity under the heavens."

Chapter 7 Food for Thought

Even though this is a chapter about business happenings, there are points here that can be applied to your life. Even though we found ourselves amid the worst health pandemic in over 100 years, we endured. We believed in our concept and ultimately helped people all over Northwest Arkansas and beyond.

1. Can you think of something you survived in your life, regardless of the obstacles you faced?

____

____

____

2. What drove you to continue despite those obstacles?

A____

____

B____

____

3. Just like Isiah 4:10 says above, is there something in your life that you have been struggling with that needs to be turned over to God?

---

4. Like Ecclesiastes 3:1 says so beautifully, Emily and I knew it was time to listen to what God was telling us and move on from Snack Lab to another "season" in our lives.

The word "season" comes from the Hebrew word zeman, which means "fixed or appointed time". The verse is a reminder that life is cyclical, and that God orchestrates time. It reassures believers that life's events are part of a divinely appointed order, not random.

Can you think of something in your life that God is leading you toward or away from? Pray for God's guidance and grace.

Chapter 8
The wonderful thing about Tiggers… is
Tiggers are wonderful things

Occasionally, Debbie likes to go to the casino. It's only a forty-five-minute drive, so she can spend a few hours there and get home before dark. She mostly plays slot machines and, more than anything, loves the lights and sounds of the machines. She only plays penny and quarter machines, so I never worry about her gambling beyond her means nd watch our life savings being gobbled down by a dazzling machine. Debbie sets a fixed budget for each visit, not with the aim of winning big, but to see how long she can make her money last while enjoying the game.! She might say, "I put $20 in the machine and played for over an hour!" Debbie has a very eccentric way of looking at life, and it's endearing in so many ways!

The other day, Debbie convinced me somehow to go to the casino with her. We were only there for about four hours, so I could handle that short of a stint. I don't like slot machines—they're boring to me—but I enjoy blackjack in short spurts. They had a $5 minimum bet per hand, so I could last a few hours playing at that rate. I made my way to the only $5 minimum table in the casino and sat down for what ended up being about two hours. As I started to get involved in the table, a gentleman came up and sat down. He handed the dealer $500 in cash and asked for chips. As he handed it over, he said, "I know I'm going to lose it all, but what the hell."

I thought to myself, *That's kind of a strange comment*, but little did I know it would continue. For about 20 minutes, with every hand, this pessimist would give us all a full diatribe of negative comments. When his two cards added up to 12 (by the way, 21 is the goal, but not over), he said, "Go ahead and give me a face card (worth 10) and take all my money." When he got two cards that equaled 10 and doubled down (doubling his bet), he would say, "Here, let me give you twice as much money—you're going to take it all anyway." This went on and on. When his $500 ran out in about 15–20 minutes, he got up and left. My thought was, *Thank goodness he's gone.*

Much to my dismay, guess who came back in about 10–15 minutes? That's right—Mr. "Doom and Gloom"! Handing the dealer another $500, he muttered, "Well, here's another $500 you can steal from me." After twenty more minutes, his personality and money were gone again—but he wasn't through. Four times (that I know of) that day, he invaded our table with his lovely personality. When he left—broke again—for the fourth time, the dealer said, "I wish he would quit coming here. He does this two to three times per week, loses tons of money, and leaves everyone in a bad mood."

Think about that—he lost $2,000 that day, and he does this two to three times per week! I have to say, I won about $200 in those two hours of play, and I refused to let our negative friend ruin my day.

When I play blackjack, my favorite part of the experience is observing people—a wide array of people with all kinds of personalities. I must say, however, this "Negative Nancy" takes the cake! As I was sitting there, I thought, *What a perfect example of Eeyore for the book.*

Life Lesson #8: Be a Positive, Fun Person Every Day

Everybody knows one... there is usually one in every office in America. It doesn't take more than 10 seconds of watching them walk in the door to recognize them. I call them "Eeyore," and they have a very contagious disease. If you don't watch out, you can catch it too—the "Eeyore Disease"!

I'm sure all of you have seen the A.A. Milne books and cartoons about *Winnie-the-Pooh* and his cast of friends in the Hundred Acre Wood. I want to focus on two main characters—Eeyore and Tigger.

Eeyore

Eeyore is a donkey who is always weary and pessimistic about life. He walks around with his slumped shoulders and his head low, sauntering slowly from one place to another. He says things in a downtrodden voice like:

- *"It isn't mine. Then again, few things are."*
- *"Not much of a house. Just right for not much of a donkey."*
- *"End of the road... nothing to do... and no hope of things getting better."*
- *"Boring—sounds like Saturday night at my house."*

Tell the truth—you've already placed your finger on the person, haven't you? Maybe that person is a friend or a relative of yours. Every time you call them, they let you know "how tired they are," "how much they have done that day," and just "how bad their life is." Kind of makes you want to crawl into a dark room and cry, doesn't it?

They are what you call "Life Vacuums"—they suck the life right out of the room!

Randy Pausch, the late professor who gave the single greatest speech I have ever seen, *The Last Lecture*, had this to say about the "Life Vacuums":

"I've never understood pity and self-pity as an emotion. We have a finite amount of time. Whether short or long, it doesn't matter. Life is to be lived."

Don't get me wrong—I'm not saying I've never felt sorry for myself or held a "pity party" from time to time. The thing you *can't* do is make it a lifestyle. Life is too short to go around miserable!

TIGGER

"Tigger" is a tiger in the Hundred Acre Wood. He is constantly in motion, excited, and eternally optimistic. "Tigger" bounces around on his tail (don't you wish you could do that?) and says things like:

"Sure! Come on, try it! It makes ya feel just grrreat!"

"The wonderful thing about Tiggers / Is Tiggers are wonderful things / Their tops are made out of rubber / Their bottoms are made out of springs / They're bouncy, trouncy, flouncy, pouncy, fun, fun, fun, fun, fun / But the most wonderful thing about Tiggers is I'm the only one / I'm the only one!"

You know what's great? The moment I mention "Tigger," someone in your life instantly comes to mind. And just like that, you're smiling. That person is always full of energy, radiating positivity with a cheerful smile. They attract people because—guess what?—they are simply fun to be around!

Today, make a point to stand up tall, straighten your shoulders, and add a little bounce to your step! Treat people with that "Tigger" excitement for what is to come. Once again, life is short, and if you're going to go around, you might as well go around happy!

LIFE IS ALL IN HOW YOU LOOK AT IT

What do you think when you look at a jalapeño pepper? Some people think only "HOT, HOT, HOT"—stay away, be careful! Others think, *Yum! A great-tasting, flavorful veggie!* Me? I LOVE IT! Think about it—it's the same pepper, so what's the difference?

Is either person wrong to think the way they do? Obviously not. Our experiences in life greatly mould the perception of how we see the world. But more importantly: How we see life greatly affects how we experience it every day:

- Do you see laws as restrictions that hold us back or as protections that create opportunities for growth?
- Do you see food as something to gorge on or as a gift from God that fuels our body every day?
- Do you see people as generally hateful and selfish, or do you believe that most people want to do the right thing and that our country was built on the backs of such individuals?

- Do you see exercise as something you *hate* to do but *have* to, or do you see it as a blessing that helps you feel better every day?

- Do you believe that friends and family who voted differently than you did are ignorant, uneducated, or uncaring? Or is it possible that people on both sides of the political debate love this country and want what's best for everyone?

Yes, how you see life is the key to happiness. Believe me, when I say that every day is a blessing, every person you meet is struggling—just like you—to do their best, and every breath you take is another opportunity to grow and improve. Even more, every day is a chance to help others achieve their dreams.

Romans 15:12-14

12 And again, Isaiah says, "The Root of Jesse will spring up, one who will arise to rule over the nations; in him, the Gentiles will hope." 13 May the God of hope fill you with all joy and peace as you trust in Him so that you may overflow with hope by the power of the Holy Spirit. 14 I myself am convinced, my brothers and sisters, that you are full of goodness, filled with knowledge, and competent to instruct one another.

Life comes at us fast and in many ways, doesn't it? How do we juggle all the demands and keep our sanity? Do you see life as just a series of events happening *to* you, making joy an unachievable goal? Or do you see each day as a gift—a chance to grow and make a difference in someone's life?

Through struggles and successes, one thing I have learned is this: life is what you make it. If you allow worldly values to dictate your happiness, you are in for a lifetime of disappointment and pain.

I challenge you to try this for a week:

- Every morning when you wake up and look in the mirror— SMILE! Look at the life that God has blessed you with today, and smile! If you allow it, your day will be brighter.
- Then, record something positive or exciting that happened in your life that day.

At the end of seven days, you will be on your way to a brighter, more positive life. Not every day will be "Tigger-worthy," but your perspective on happiness will change!

"When you have once seen the glow of happiness on the face of a beloved person, you know that a man can have no vocation but to awaken that light on the faces surrounding him. In the depth of winter, I finally learned that within me there lay an invincible summer."

—Albert Camus

Chapter 8 Food for Thought

Chapter 8 Challenge:

Take the Daily "Smile Challenge" from above.

Every morning when you get up and look in the mirror- SMILE! Look at the life that God has blessed you with today, and smile! If you allow it, your day will be brighter! Then record something positive or exciting that happened in your life that day.

At the end of 7 days, you will be on your way to a brighter, more positive life. Not every day will be "Tigger worthy", but your perspective on happiness will change!

Sunday______________________________________

____

Monday______________________________________

____

Tuesday______________________________________

____

Wednesday______________________________________

____

Thursday______________________________________

Friday _______________________________________

Saturday _______________________________________

1. Re-read Romans 15:12-14 above. How does that passage impact you?

A_______________________________________

____

B_______________________________________

____

2. **Challenge #2**- "Attack" an Eeyore with positivity! I challenge you to spend some time with that person this week and let them know about anything positive that person does. Make sure they know they are of value.

____

____

____

____

****

Chapter 9
One Hundred Shades of Gray

Proverbs 28:26

"Those who trust in themselves are fools, but those who walk in wisdom are kept safe."

One defining trait of teenagers and young adults stepping out of high school and college is this: everything is black or white—it's either GREAT or TERRIBLE. It's either 100% right or downright wrong. When I walked out of high school, I thought I knew everything—just ask me! After college, with a little more experience and a lot more education, I merely thought I might know everything. Boy, was I wrong on both counts! Life isn't always black and white; the truth often lies in the gray areas. In fact, it's in those gray areas where we find common sense and the ability to solve problems. The longer I live, the more I realize I don't know everything—but I do know how to solve problems.

Life Lesson #9: Everything in life is not black or white. In-between lies a lot of gray—and that's usually where common sense is found.

Good judgment comes from experience, and experience comes from bad judgment.

If this statement is true, and we measure wisdom by the mistakes that eventually lead to good judgment, then I must be a genius by now! I don't come from the "School of Hard Knocks" because I have been very blessed in my life. Rather, I think I come from the "School of Stupidity." My ability to make good judgments has literally come from experiencing the consequences of bad decisions! The longer I live, the more I realize how little I actually know.

My health is no exception. I can't sit here and say I didn't know any better than to eat all the wrong foods for 50 years—that would be a lie! Now that I've studied healthy living and experienced its benefits firsthand, I obviously know more than I did before. But let's be honest—I KNEW what I was eating wasn't good for me. I KNEW that neglecting consistent exercise would eventually lead to health problems. The simple fact is, I valued the wrong things. I valued eating unhealthy foods more than I valued my health, and I valued my free time more than I valued exercising. It really is that simple.

One valuable lesson I have learned is this: keep dipping your toe into the waters of life and use your best judgment. The most important thing? If you fail, learn from it. Common sense will guide the way.

Through experience, I've found that only a few things are true 100% of the time:

- God loves you no matter what.
- Your family—whatever that family looks like, blood-related or not—is the most important group of people in your life.
- When you're sick, everybody wants their mom. (That just made me cry!)
- Nobody is happy at every moment of their life.
- No matter how good you are at something, there is always someone better. No matter what record was just broken, someone will come along and break it.
- It's true that life is not fair.
- And finally, there is not enough sauce or seasoning in the world to make liver taste good! (Sorry, that's just my opinion.) There are people who like liver—but they might be psychos!

Common sense is not something we are born with—though I've met a few people who might make you question that theory! I believe common sense is mostly acquired through experience. The more of life we engage with, the more we grow, especially at a young age. As we discussed in Chapter 7, a large percentage of the young people we interviewed and hired at Snack Lab lacked basic common sense in so many areas. To them, everything was black and white; they had no concept of how one thing in life affects another.

I had some of those same traits as a kid, but not to this extreme. The real issue is what these kids have—or haven't—been exposed to growing up. Many came to us at sixteen or eighteen needing a little money, but the problem wasn't just that they had never had a job—it was that they had never worked at all! Their parents hadn't required them to clean their rooms, make their beds, rake the leaves, mow the yard, do the dishes, or do anything resembling actual work. Hence, they knew nothing about responsibility. On the flip side, if we hired a young person who had done chores most of their life, they quickly adapted to what we needed from them. Many teachers have told me the same thing—parents expect schools to teach their kids everything.

Here's a fact: if you aren't teaching your kids to love reading and learning, they won't get it at school. Teachers do all they can, but ultimately, it is the parents' responsibility to imbue in a love of learning. Parents must also teach their kids to brush their teeth well, take responsibility for their actions, and develop a strong work ethic. Teach your kids the value of hard work and the satisfaction of completing a task—their future employers and spouses will thank you!

Ever been around someone and thought, *He just gets it?* That's a person with common sense. Ever known someone you can always trust to ask for advice? That's a person with common sense. Ever solved a problem and thought, *Why didn't I think of that in the first place?* That's common sense finally prevailing

When my daughter Anna was fifteen, she began distancing herself from certain friends who were getting into trouble. (Clearly, she was much smarter than I was at that age!) She told me, "I can still be friends with them, but I don't have to hang around them." I nearly passed out from the sheer wisdom contained in that one statement! Thank goodness she takes after her mother!

One thing to understand is this: every person matures at their own pace.

Anna had a level of maturity as a young teenager that you don't see very often. Our two boys, however, matured much later—MUCH later! But all three of our kids understood that they were responsible for their own decisions, even from a young age. I'm very proud of all of them, and I know the common sense they've developed will serve them well throughout their lives. I pray every day that they pass on that same wisdom and experience to their own children.

We're all guilty of a lack of common sense from time to time. Often, our passion for something overrides logic. That doesn't mean it always ends badly, but it does mean we need to set foot into such situations with our eyes wide open. When I started Snack Lab, I knew the smartest financial decision would have been to hold onto my money and keep investing in my retirement. However, my passion for helping people live healthier lifestyles was too strong to ignore.

That doesn't mean I was wrong to start Snack Lab. I knew the risks. I didn't know we would face the worst global health crisis in over a century, nor did I foresee many of the challenges that would arise. But sometimes, when your heart is in the right place, following it is never the wrong choice.

"All truth, in the long run, is only common sense clarified."

—Thomas Huxley

How Do You Solve Problems?

There isn't a one-size-fits-all answer to solving problems. The best approach depends on several factors:

1. **Who does it impact?** (Family, friends, customers, your boss, or others?)
2. **What does your gut say?**
3. **What does your heart say?** (*By the way, if your gut and heart are in alignment, go for it!*)
4. **What will it cost you?** (Money, relationships, time, or other valuable things?)
5. **What will you gain?**

How Do You Decide the Answers?

1. Prayer should always be the first response.
2. Consult those who may be affected by your decision.

3. Examine all the facts, then balance them against your gut and heart—this is where common sense comes in.

4. Recognize that not every decision has a clear "right" or "wrong" answer.

o Some choices are black and white—when that's the case, the answer is obvious.

o However, many decisions fall into a gray area. The key is this: once you decide, don't look back.

o Commit to your choice with all your heart. It's not about making the "right" or "wrong" decision—it's about owning *your* decision.

Chapter 9 Food for Thought

1. Chapter 9 Challenge:

The next time you have a decision to make, call a family meeting (or call together a group of your friends). Lay out the following for them:

1. The facts and both sides of the decision you need to make.
2. Your gut reaction to the issue.
3. Your heart reaction to the issue.

Then, lead the group in a prayer for discernment. After the prayer, ask each person for their opinion. Just listen intently.

Listen to each and understand that each person has your best interest at heart. However, in the end, make the decision your heart and common sense tell you to do.

After everyone has spoken, tell them your decision and explain why you made it.

Share your thoughts about this exercise:

____

____

____

2. Re-read Proverbs 28:26 above. How does that passage impact you?

____

____

____

****

Chapter 10
Bite Me

Of course, you knew this was coming—a chapter about eating the right foods as part of a healthy lifestyle. After all, I am a Certified Holistic Health Coach! Well, here goes:

Life Lesson #10: Eat the food that God grows.

FOOD IS MEDICINE

Houston… we have a problem. There is no real healthcare in America anymore—it's "sick care." Many inflammatory diseases are preventable and, in many cases, even reversible. Yet, we mostly just "manage" them with medications. Don't get me wrong—I'm not blaming doctors for this dilemma. They are doing the only thing they can in most situations. Somewhere along the way, we have forgotten to take responsibility for our own bodies.

It's just easier this way... High blood pressure? Pop in some pills. That's fine, but what about changing the eating habits that caused the high blood pressure in the first place? Pre-diabetes? Just take some Metformin. How about NOT eating donuts for breakfast?

In my opinion, it's not just what we eat today that causes the problem—it's also what we don't eat. Folks, processed food is only partially food. Some of it may contain actual food ingredients, but much of it is manufactured in a lab. On the other hand, whole, naturally grown and raised foods have the power to heal. The nutrition, fiber, and natural goodness in these foods are amazing! Whole, natural food is medicine.

So why do we eat "junk food" that causes inflammation and breeds disease in our bodies? And why do companies keep shoving it down our throats? Here are some reasons:

1. We are busy—convenient, fast foods may not be the most nutritious, but they are easy.
2. Many people have lost the love for cooking and using their imaginations in the kitchen.
3. Sometimes, we simply don't know any better.
4. There's more money to be made in "disease care" than in "well care," so little is done to curb the spread of inflammatory diseases.

It's time to understand that whole foods—the ones God designed for us—are truly the best medicine. Give your body a chance to function the way God intended.

Psalm 104:14

"He makes grass grow for the cattle, and plants for people to cultivate—bringing forth food from the earth."

1 Corinthians 6:19-20

"Do you not know that your bodies are temples of the Holy Spirit?... Therefore, honor God with your bodies."

The question I would ask you is this: Are you honoring God's temple with the food and drinks you consume every day? I know I wasn't for the first 53 years of my life. Believe it or not, my gluttonous ways were a point of pride as a child. Joey Chestnut had nothing on me! I could eat more food—and faster—than anyone, especially steak!

One weekend, some of my 21-year-old friends and I loaded into a van and drove to Tulsa specifically to eat at a restaurant called *Cattle Rustlers*. It wasn't just a steakhouse—it was famous for its "All-You-Can-Eat Steak" menu. They brought each of us a salad, baked potato, toast, and an 8-ounce sirloin steak. As long as we kept asking, they kept bringing another 8-ounce sirloin to our table. We all just told them to keep them coming! This went on for quite a while, and let's just say a LOT of steaks were served that night. I won't reveal how many, but suffice it to say, we were all pigs that evening!

As you might suspect, *Cattle Rustlers* went out of business less than a year later. My steak-eating habits, however, continued for the next 30 years! That led to an outrageously high cholesterol number that should have killed me. You might say, "Well, God made cattle, so what's wrong with eating beef?" The answer is—nothing unless you treat it like your best friend and spend all your time with it.

To be honest, I've been a vegan for the past 8–9 years, and it has served me well. However, there's nothing wrong with including meat in your diet. As I've mentioned, I lost most of my weight while still eating meat. The real problem is the quantity of meat we consume in the U.S. Your body can only properly digest meat in three-ounce portions at a time. The main reason I quit eating meat? Three ounces is just enough to tick me off! I cringe when I see the oversized portions of meat offered in restaurants today.

Healthy Eating Tips

80/20 Rule

1. Ensure that 80% of your plate consists of vibrant colors—green, red, orange, and bright yellow. Eat the rainbow!
2. Cook with fresh ingredients 80% of the time—avoid packaged, processed, boxed, or canned foods.
3. Prepare meals at home at least 80% of the time.
4. Stop eating when you feel about 80% full.

Focus on Reduction Techniques

1. Use smaller plates and bowls—serve yourself half of your usual portion.
2. Avoid drinking beverages while eating meals.
3. Chew each bite thoroughly and savor the flavors.
4. Drink a glass of water or eat an apple 10–15 minutes before a meal to curb hunger.

The crazy thing is that the world is so crazy when it comes to eating, dieting, and our overall relationship with food. If we relied solely on commercials, we'd believe:

- A highly processed cereal loaded with preservatives and sugar is actually good for heart health.
- Energy shots are superior to coffee and are even doctor-recommended.
- Frosted Mini Wheats improve children's attentiveness by 20%—seriously?
- A fruit juice company's claim that their juice reduces the risk of heart disease, prostate cancer, and erectile dysfunction.
- "Less sugar" means a product is healthier when, in reality, manufacturers often add more processed fats to maintain flavor.
- Chips labeled as having "less salt" today still contain three times the salt of a regular chip from 30 years ago.

We are being led down a path of poor health by masterful food marketers who understand that adding more sugar, salt, or fat to a product makes us crave it—and buy more. But let's be clear: these marketing wizards aren't evil; they're simply doing their job. The responsibility lies with us. We must use our common sense, as discussed in the previous chapter, to uncover the real truth.

God's Nutritional Blueprint

Every time God creates food, it is nutritionally dense and healthy. Every food produced in a factory or laboratory is a ticking time bomb for our health.

When it comes to stocking your kitchen with healthy foods, reading labels is a prerequisite. However, even the most informed shoppers can be hoodwinked by deceptive claims on packaging—and that's intentional. The truth is that even food labels lie. Food marketing preys on our emotions, leading us to buy cleverly disguised junk masquerading as health food.

At Snack Lab, I had customers constantly asking for items to fit their latest diet trends:

- Low-carb
- Low-fat
- Sugar-free
- Fasting
- Juice cleanses
- Calorie counting
- And countless others

While it's laudable that people want to improve their health, most are going about it the wrong way. Fixating on calories, carbs, fats, or points is a self-defeating cycle. You cannot deprive your body of essential nutrients and expect sustainable improvement. It just won't work.

A few years ago, I wrote a paper about the "Low Carb Theory," which I still refer to often. Let's break it down.

Good Carbs vs. Bad Carbs

Many diets promote "no carbs" or "low carbs," but there's a lot of fallacy out there. Let's examine carbohydrates—what's beneficial and what's harmful?

Good Carbs:

These come from whole, natural, nutrient-dense foods, such as:

- Broccoli
- Cauliflower
- Butternut squash
- Green apples
- Carrots
- Sweet potatoes & many more

Bad Carbs:

Bad carbs are refined, processed, and man-made. If it's popped, puffed, flaked, shredded, or instant, it has been refined. The so-called "whole grain" bread, pasta, and high-fiber cereals made from multiple grains? They are all refined!

Bad carbs are calorie-dense but lack essential micronutrients. You can consume a large number of calories from bad carbs yet never truly nourish your body. Take a look at this comparison:

103 Calories of Sweet Potatoes	103 Calories of Unenriched Wheat Bread (1 slice)
24g carbohydrates	20g carbohydrates
4g dietary fiber	1g dietary fiber
438% RDA for Vitamin A	0% RDA for Vitamin A
37% RDA for Vitamin C	0% RDA for Vitamin C
14% RDA for Calcium	0% RDA for Calcium
17% RDA for Iron	1% RDA for Iron

As you can see, despite having nearly the same calorie count, sweet potatoes provide significantly more nutrition than so-called "healthy" wheat bread.

Don't every let anyone tell you to reduce all carbs. What you are looking to do is reduce BAD carbs!

Another example:

- **Bad Carbs:** 4 teaspoons of white sugar contain 60 calories of pure carbohydrates—no nutrients whatsoever. This is why they're called "empty calories."
- **Good Carbs:** 1 cup of cooked broccoli contains about 60 carbohydrate calories but also provides Vitamin B, phosphorus, magnesium, iron, copper, manganese, zinc, chromium, Vitamin C, Vitamin K, Vitamin E, folate, potassium, beta-carotene, calcium, and selenium—the exact micronutrients your body needs to metabolize those carbs.

The Key Takeaways for Healthy Eating

1. **Eat what God provides.**
   - As Psalms reminds us, God created the human body and then provided perfectly suited foods to sustain it. Have faith in His provision.

2. **Replace sweets and processed foods with whole, natural foods.**

o   Eliminate processed sugars entirely.

3. **Limit meat consumption to no more than 3 ounces per meal.**

4. **Reduce or eliminate store-bought bread and crackers.**

5. **Stop drinking your calories.**

o   Avoid high-calorie and sugary drinks. Stick to water, tea, or black coffee. Aim to drink half of your body weight (in ounces) of water each day. For example, if you weigh 160 lbs., strive for 80 ounces of water daily.

Final Thoughts

The secret to lasting weight loss and improved health isn't found in dieting—it's in transforming your lifestyle—a 180-degree turn. This is a journey, not a quick fix. If you have a bad day, don't be discouraged. Focus on small, consistent improvements. If you commit to doing your best and letting your body function as it was designed, you'll see results. And always remember: meaningful change starts in the heart.

Chapter 10 Food for Thought

1. **Chapter 10 Challenge**:

For one day, I want you to eat only fresh food—nothing in a pouch, can, or bag, unless it is only food that God grew. Frozen veggies are okay but with no sauce added. Only fresh meat, fresh veggies, and fresh fruit. One day. At the end of the day, write down how you feel and your thoughts.

____

____

____

2. Re-read 1 Corinthians 6:19-20 above. How does that conflict with what you have been eating?

____

____

____

3.   What needs to change to honor that verse?

____

____

____

Chapter 11
Move it!

Here we go again! I was a sophomore in high school, and for some crazy reason, I wanted to play football. Maybe it was because I had spent my entire life watching Razorback Football and Rogers Mountie Football. Maybe it was because EVERY healthy male in Rogers played football. Maybe it was because I was the biggest kid in my class, and I didn't really have a choice. Whatever the reason—probably a combination of all the above—I loved it!

Very few sophomores got to play on the varsity team—if at all—at our school. I was a second-team offensive lineman, backing up a senior. Looking back now, he wasn't very good, so what did that make me? We had just finished the hardest training I had ever experienced at that point in my life. I thought I was going to die every day at practice during two-a-days.

Two-a-days, as they called them, were the first two weeks of practice before school started. We had two grueling two-hour practices each day. After those, we still had to do agility drills and wind sprints. Our practice field was in the parking lot near the game field—rocky, with patches of dirt, a little grass, and, later in the season, shards of broken glass from cars running over them. We got one water break per practice, which meant sprinting 100 yards to line up for a drink from a single water hose. The line was so long that by the time the slower guys (like me) got there, the whistle would blow, and we had to sprint back to practice. The coaches didn't consider a practice complete unless at least one player threw up—usually more. My personal victory that season? Surviving every practice without throwing up!

As sophomores on the JV team, we quickly figured out our role. Varsity games were on Friday nights (think *Friday Night Lights!*), and JV games were on Monday nights. Monday afternoons, we practiced with the varsity for two hours, then suited up to play in the JV game. We learned this the hard way. Our first varsity game was against

Springdale, and we lost 34-0. Our high school had always been competitive, so this loss wasn't acceptable to our coaches. They took it out on us. After two hours of practice with the varsity, we endured what they called "Loser's Practice"—another 90 minutes of 100-yard agility drills and wind sprints. By the end of that three-and-a-half-hour massacre, we lay on the ground, barely breathing. Then came the final blow: coaches proclaimed, "Sophomores, get dressed for your JV game. Game starts in 30 minutes!" I'm not exaggerating—this is exactly how it happened.

I don't recall how I played that night, but I do remember that we won. I think we were too afraid to lose! Our senior-heavy varsity team struggled that year, which meant several more "Loser's Practices." Later in the season, about 15 seniors were kicked off the team for off-the-field issues, allowing a handful of us sophomores to start the next Friday night game against Conway. I don't remember much of that game—probably because on the very first play, I was knocked silly by Conway's all-state defensive tackle. I played the entire game but don't recall any of it. That was my first and only concussion in football, and it was certainly *not* memorable.

That season was my introduction to serious physical training. After those brutal workouts, everything else felt easy by comparison. I dreaded those wind sprints and agility drills, but somewhere along the way, I developed a love for working out—in a somewhat masochistic way. Over the next five to six years, my routine included running, weightlifting, swimming, and other training. It was always tough, but it was also fun. There was something special about going through that torture with teammates—it created a bond I'll always treasure.

But what happens to your fitness routine when the team sport ends? When you enter the real world, balancing work and college? When you meet the love of your life, get married, and three years later start having babies? What happens when you're coaching all three kids in their sports while working full-time? When your kids start searching for colleges, and you spend weekends driving them across the country to find the right fit?

I'll tell you what happens—working out, or as busy adults call it, "exercising," takes a back seat to everything else. At least, it did for me. I joined every new gym in town but never went more than once. I tried every diet known to man, only to end up heavier than when I started. I kept eating like a 10,000-calorie-burning college athlete, always promising myself that *next week* I'd start fresh. But the next week turned into the next, and the next, and the next.

If you're a high school or college athlete, your workouts will be intense and relentless. But what most people don't realize is that a regular person doesn't need to punish your body to stay healthy—you just need to *keep moving*. It's what we call an "active, healthy lifestyle." The key is consistency. Any kind of movement for at least 30 minutes a day is enough. Good heart health doesn't require brutal training sessions—it only takes getting your heart rate about 15% above its resting rate for 20 minutes. That means 10 minutes to get it there and 20 minutes to maintain it, so at least 30 minutes' total. The type of exercise doesn't matter—running, swimming, biking, walking, yoga—just move.

Nike had it right:

JUST DO IT!

Life Lesson #11 - Spend time each day engaging in movement to maintain an active, healthy lifestyle.

Do you want your body to be like a pond or a river?

I was riding my bike the other day (before the weather turned cold) and passed a pond on some farmland. The water didn't look good at all—it was stagnant, with green patches around the edges. The water was dark and murky, almost uninviting. Later that day, I was looking at some photos from our trip to Colorado and came across a picture of a beautiful mountain river—clean, briskly flowing, and vibrant. Immediately, I thought about how much healthier that river water looked compared to the pond water.

As I've mentioned before, about 70% of your body is made up of water. Daily exercise gets that water moving and prevents stagnation. Think about that pond—over time, its still water becomes covered in slime and gunk, a breeding ground for disease and toxins. That's exactly what happens inside the body when there's no movement. But when water moves and flows, life thrives. Running water is fresher, cleaner, and full of energy.

That is exactly what exercise does! It refreshes your body, clears out toxins and bacteria, sharpens your mind, and increases your energy levels. The more the water inside your body moves and circulates, the better your overall health.

Remember, though, you must replace the water you lose by staying hydrated with fresh, clean water.

In the Bible, flowing water is often associated with life and healing. Exercise creates movement in your body, keeping you refreshed, strong, and healthy. It is a powerful remedy for preventing disease and maintaining vitality. So, how about stirring the waters in your body today? **Get moving!**

Once I began my health journey and lost a significant amount of weight, I was able to walk consistently. Eventually, I progressed to running and swimming. After 45 years of not riding a bike, I decided to take it up again so I could enter a local triathlon. I competed in my first *Trifest for MS Triathlon* and managed to finish—though I probably needed a calendar more than a stopwatch! I didn't finish last, but let's just say the competition was close behind me.

To improve my triathlon performance at 54 years old, I joined a gym—and this time, I actually went every day! The gym, called GPP, had an incredible community that helped me regain the strength I had lost during my weight loss journey. I also worked with an endurance coach to learn more about triathlon training.

After competing in several triathlons, I realized that running was no longer a sustainable option for me. Years of football had left me with knee injuries that made extensive run training difficult. That led me to explore *Aqua Bike* races, which are triathlons without the running—just swimming and biking. It turned out to be an exciting and rewarding alternative. I even completed two Half-Ironman Aqua Bikes, which involved a one-mile open water swim and a 56-mile bike ride.

Considering that I once weighed 400 pounds and struggled with multiple health issues, I am incredibly proud of how far I've come. I was never the fastest athlete, but that was never the point. As Nike says—**I just did it!**

Hey buddy, grow a pair!

I had an interesting experience this weekend, competing in Border Wars 1/2 Ironman Triathlon and Aqua Bike in St. Louis. The swim was in an off shoot of the Mississippi River, and the bike was along the river bottom area. I showed up early to check in and check-out the course on Saturday morning, the day before the race. IT WAS FREEZING COLD on Saturday all over, and St. Louis was no exception. When I got there on Saturday morning, it was 42 degrees, and the wind was blowing about 40 miles per hour (no exaggeration!). I made my way down to the river to look at the swim area, and I have to say, I was not really excited about the opportunity ahead of me tomorrow. As I said, it was 42 degrees outside with 40 MPH winds, and the river was white capping unbelievably. To top that, as you can imagine, the water was dark brown muddy (duh- the muddy Mississippi), and it turned out the water was 55 degrees! These are not ideal conditions, even for a polar bear!!

As I walked down to the water, there was one other person there, and it turns out to be a woman from Wisconsin who was competing tomorrow as well. We were talking about the conditions, and I made the comment, "To be honest, I'm not sure I really want to do this thing tomorrow if it's going to be like this."   I will never forget her reply to me: "HEY BUDDY, SOUNDS LIKE YOU NEEED TO GROW A PAIR! YOU DIDN'T COME ALL THE WAY UP HERE TO "WUSS OUT" DID YOU?" To be fair, she didn't exactly say *"wuss,"* but you get the idea.

At first, I was taken aback. But the more I thought about it, the more I realized she was right. They don't promise perfect conditions for these events. If I wanted to be an endurance athlete, I had to tough it out.

Race day was still brutally cold, but thankfully, the wind had calmed down. As I started my swim in the 55-degree water, I entertained more than one thought of flagging down a lifeguard to paddle me back to shore. My hands and feet were frozen, and the river water tasted awful. But every time I wanted to quit, I heard that woman's voice in my head: *"Sounds like you need to grow a pair!"* Whether she realized it or not, her words pushed me through that swim.

The fact is, if you want to improve—whether in fitness, career, or life—you have to push through moments of extreme discomfort. In fact, you should embrace them. Those moments shape you into a stronger, more resilient person. I don't know if they'll literally help you *grow a pair,* but they'll definitely help you grow.

By the way, that race was my second Half Aqua Bike of the year, and I finished **1 hour and 8 minutes faster** than my first. Maybe "growing a pair" really does work!

Jeremiah 29:11-13

"For I know the plans I have for you," declares the Lord, "plans for welfare and not for evil, to give you a future and a hope. Then you will call upon me and come and pray to me, and I will hear you. You will seek me and find me when you seek me with all your heart."

Final Thought: Take Your Exercise Outside!

The last piece of advice I want to share is this: **whenever possible, exercise outdoors.** Being outside exposes you to fresh air, natural light, and vitamin D, which all contribute to better health. While it might be easier to hop on a stationary bike or elliptical, nothing compares to walking, running, or cycling in nature.

Even cold weather shouldn't be a deterrent—just dress appropriately, and you'll be fine. Find a time of day that works for you and make movement a part of your daily routine. Do it because it's fun. Do it because it's good for you. **You'll be glad you did!**

Chapter 11 Food for Thought

- **<u>Chapter 11 Challenge</u>:**

No matter the level of exercise you are currently experiencing, I want you to challenge yourself this coming week to "move" every day! For at least 30 minutes each day, I want you to try a different movement and see what works for you.

Log your thoughts for each day:

Sunday_______________________________________

____

____

Monday_______________________________________

____

____

Tuesday_______________________________________

____

____

Wednesday_____________________________________

____

____

Thursday____

____

____

Friday____

____

____

Saturday____

____

____

- Make a commitment on what movement you can achieve each day going forward. Remember- just 30 minutes or more each day:

____

____

____

- Re-read Jeremiah 29:11-13 above. How does it fit in with an active, healthy lifestyle?

____

____

____

****

Chapter 12
Light the Fire!

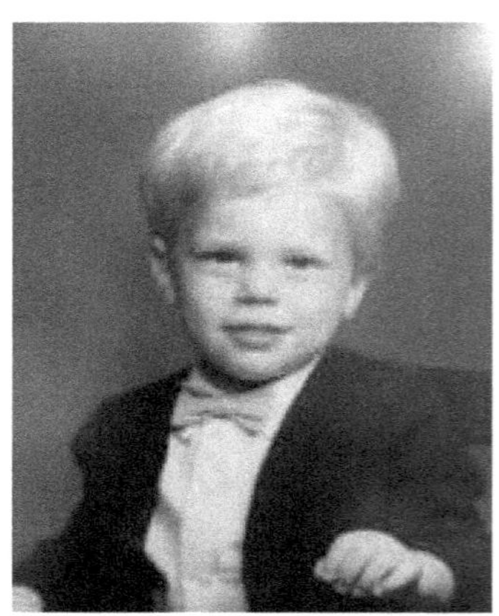

When I was a kid, I learned a lesson about never quitting—delivered, of all things, by an ant!

I grew up in a wooded area in Rogers, so it wasn't unusual to see a "wood ant" in the house—it was inevitable. One day, I was taking an unusually long shower (which was fun as a kid but drove me crazy when my own kids did it as a parent!). As I stood there, I noticed an ant climbing up the tile wall. He was working diligently, trying to reach something at the top. Being a typical boy, I had other plans. Just as he got three-quarters of the way up, I knocked him back down.

I watched as he started climbing again—without hesitation. Time after time, he just kept going, no matter what. Finally, after one last knock, he got caught in the drain, and I never saw him again. But I like to believe that even after landing in the septic tank, he started his climb again, never quitting.

It was a small moment, but somehow, that tiny, determined ant stuck with me. I hadn't intended to learn anything from that silly experience, but the lesson stayed with me for years. That ant showed me what true perseverance looks like.

What impressed me most wasn't just that he refused to quit—it was that he never hesitated. The moment he fell, he immediately started climbing again. He knew what he wanted and wasn't going to let a little slip deter it from its goal.

Dedication and focus aren't just for ants and spiders. My first boss, Whitey Smith, used to say, "Bland, try using your head for something besides a hat rack!" Use your brain, but more importantly, use your heart to create positive motivation in your life. Our hearts aren't there to limit our growth—follow your heart to your future.

Seek the truth, no matter where it **leads.** Be the chess player, not the chess piece. It's easy to follow the crowd without thinking, but it doesn't lead to true happiness. Take charge of your life, make your own decisions, and let those choices create good in the world around you.

Life Lesson #12: Find What You're Passionate About and Go for It!

This chapter is about discovering your passion and sticking with it—just like that ant. But where does passion come from?

The other day, I heard the song *Eye of the Tiger* on the radio. One verse caught my attention:

So many times, it happens too fast

You trade your passion for glory

Don't lose your grip on the dreams of the past

You must fight just to keep them alive.

It's easy to get distracted by what the world offers, isn't it? Have you ever felt like you've traded your passion for temporary rewards—money, power, status, fame, or just the never-ending busyness of life?

Consider these questions:

- What do you truly want from life?
- What is your dream?
- Are you actively pursuing it?
- What's standing in your way?

What is *The Eye of the Tiger*? To me, it's that inner fire that says, "I can do this." It's the determination that separates those who move toward their dreams from those who merely exist.

There are two ways to look at life:

1. Wake up, go to work to make a living, come home, eat dinner, talk to your family, go to bed—repeat. OR…

2. Wake up excited about the opportunity to make a difference. Go to work because you love what you do, and it's a privilege to do what's fun. Then, spend quality time with your family and go to bed eager for what tomorrow will bring.

That's the *Eye of the Tiger*—the mindset that transforms life. It's not stress that brings joy; it's the *thrill of the fight*, the challenge of rising up. Perhaps our greatest challenge is refusing to let the world dictate our ups and downs. Fight to keep your dreams alive.

Throughout my life, I've found passions that drive me forward. As a kid, it was football and sports. I loved competing, no matter the game. I played baseball, football, and basketball (until high school), and I competed in track (shot put and discus). I even loved water skiing—though it wasn't an official competition, I turned it into one. I always wanted to be the best among my friends. (I didn't say I *was* the best, but I wanted to be.)

1 Peter 4:10-11

10 *Each of you should use whatever gift you have received to serve others as faithful stewards of God's grace in its various forms.*

11 *If anyone speaks, they should do so as one who speaks the very words of God. If anyone serves, they should do so with the strength God provides, so that in all things God may be praised through Jesus Christ. To him be the glory and the power forever and ever. Amen.*

I discovered another passion as a young adult—singing. After accepting Christ at 22, I attended a Bible study in Fayetteville with many young people eager to deepen their Christian faith. One night, during a discussion on spiritual gifts, I prayed, "God, show me my gift so I can share it with others." I wasn't sure what that would look like, but I believed in the concept of spiritual gifts.

While completing my college degrees, I held several jobs. One of them was at "Y'all Come Back Saloon" in Fayetteville, a massive Country/Western-themed bar. I worked as a bouncer, spent plenty of time dancing, and even taught Country/Western dance on occasion. On weekends, thousands of people packed the place, and live bands performed regularly. Over time, we got to know the musicians well. One of the bands, "Winchester," came to town about once a month, staying for a week at a time.

One afternoon, as Winchester was rehearsing, their leader, Steve Jones, called out to me: "Bobby, come up and sing with us." I thought he was crazy, but I agreed. He asked what song I wanted to sing, and I said, "Anything by Alabama." As the band started playing "Love in the First Degree," I began to sing. Suddenly, I felt an indescribable power surge through me—it was as if I were outside my body, watching myself perform. And, to my surprise, I was pretty good! I ended up singing several Alabama songs that day, and Winchester invited me to perform with them that night at the bar. That moment sparked a lifelong love affair with singing. As I performed that night, I felt like I was walking on air.

When Debbie and I decided to get married, we planned the ceremony at the First United Methodist Church in Bentonville, her childhood church. By then, my passion for music had only deepened, and I had even written a song to sing to Debbie at our wedding. I performed it for Vicky Hollingshead, the church pianist and leader, and after hearing it, she asked if I had ever sung Christian music. I told her I hadn't. She invited me to join the church choir, which led to years of choir singing and many solo performances. I sang at weddings, funerals, and anywhere else I had the opportunity. I love all types of music, but I feel most at home when singing for the Lord.

I have been blessed to produce two full Christian music albums:

1.   **Cornerstone**
2.   **The Story**

Each album contains ten contemporary Christian songs that hold deep meaning for me. While they may not have gone gold, they were a source of great pride, and I was able to sell a respectable number of copies.

I even had a brief experience in a talent competition. At my wife's urging, I entered a local talent show just for fun. There were about twenty contestants, and for once, winning wasn't my focus—I just wanted to sing. About halfway through the show, as I waited my turn, I watched an eight-year-old girl perform "Somewhere Over the Rainbow" from *The Wizard of Oz*. She was phenomenal and sure to be a top contender. When my turn came, I sang—though I can't even remember what song I chose! I thought I did well and might be in the running for the top prize, a $400 award.

Then, the final contestant stepped onto the stage. He was accompanied by another person carrying a guitar. As he sat down, I noticed he had no arms. His assistant placed the guitar on the ground and removed his shoes and socks. What happened next was unbelievable—he began playing the guitar with his feet. It was the most incredible thing I had ever witnessed. The audience erupted into a standing ovation. At that moment, I knew my talent show days were over. He rightfully won first place, the young girl took second, and I placed third. I felt honored just to be in their company.

I truly believe my gift of song came from God, and that night, He answered my prayer. Singing has been a passion unlike any other, a blessing I pursued with love and devotion. Today, at 67, I can still sing, though not as well as I once did. Recently, I performed a solo at a funeral for a close friend's mother. It didn't sound the same as when I sang at her father's funeral years ago, but it was still God-driven, and I felt blessed to do it. God grants us talents—it is up to us to use them in His name.

"There is one quality which one must possess to win, and that is definiteness of purpose, the knowledge of what one wants, and a burning desire to possess it." —Napoleon Hill.

Another passion I discovered later in life was youth sports coaching. It began when I coached my son Jesse's fifth-grade football team. Jesse, a natural Type-A personality, was fiercely competitive and was really looking forward to playing football. Joe Murphy, the father of Jesse's best friend, and I decided to coach the team together. Jesse took to football like a duck to water, and I found myself loving the coaching experience—not just with Jesse but with all the kids. To my surprise, I had a knack for it.

When our second son, John, came along, I coached him as well. We had some great teams, and both boys excelled on the field. However, the most important lesson I wanted them to learn wasn't about winning—it was about teamwork. I wanted them to understand that playing for their teammates, not just for themselves, was what truly mattered. That kind of selflessness carries over into life—into careers, marriages, parenthood, and beyond.

As time went on, I was fortunate enough to coach all three of our kids in sports—football, basketball, baseball, and softball. One of the most rewarding experiences was coaching the Cobras, the fast-pitch softball travel team I mentioned earlier. They embodied the true spirit of teamwork, always showing up for each other, and their lives since have reflected that same camaraderie. There are countless life lessons to be learned through team sports, and I was blessed to pass those on to young athletes for many years.

Another incredible gift coaching gave me was the opportunity to mentor teams that didn't include my own kids. Over 18 years, I coached hundreds of young athletes, watching them grow—not just in skill but in character. Many went on to compete at higher levels, and even more became outstanding individuals. The passion I found in coaching was exhilarating, a true blessing from God. To this day, I still run into former players who greet me with a warm, "Hey, Coach Bobby!" What they don't realize is that they taught me just as much—if not more—than I ever taught them.

I also discovered another passion: helping others embrace a healthy, active lifestyle. That passion led to my work as a health coach and later to the creation of Snack Lab. I followed that calling, and it eventually led me here—to share this journey with you in this book.

My prayer is that you, too, find a way to pursue your passion. The key is listening to your heart, believing in God's grace, and trusting yourself enough to keep going. Your heart will tell you when the time is right—just don't stop listening.

"The two most important days in your life are the day you were born and the day you find out why." —Mark Twain

Each of us was placed on this Earth, in this exact moment, for a purpose. I have found that when I dedicate myself to helping others—whether it's singing the Lord's word, coaching young athletes, guiding my own children, or inspiring others to embrace a balanced, healthy life—my path becomes clear. When I can reach people's hearts and encourage them to walk their own paths with confidence, my own life is enriched in ways I never imagined.

My hope for you is that you, too, discover why you are here. Your purpose doesn't have to be grand or extraordinary—it just has to be real. And always remember: God is praying for you.

****

Chapter 12 Food for Thought

1. **<u>Chapter 12 Challenge</u>:**

No matter what your age, I want you to take the time in the next few weeks and pray that God will show you your gift- what God gave you. It doesn't mean you have to quit your current job and do only that. The challenge is to pray for more meaning in your life. When God shows you the answer, write it here.

____

____

____

____

2. Make a commitment on how you can use this talent that God gave you:

____

____

____

____

3. Re-read 1 Peter 4:10-11 above. What does it mean to you?

____

____

____

____

4. How have the talents God has blessed you with been used to help others at this point in your life?

____

____

____

____

****

Chapter 13
Lucky #13

Life Lesson #13 – Gratitude + Faith = Hope
Isaiah 40:31

"But those who hope in the Lord will renew their strength. They will soar on wings like eagles; they will run and not grow weary; they will walk and not be faint."

4 Pillars to a Happy, Healthy Lifestyle

1. Maintain an "Attitude of Gratitude"
2. Eat REAL food that God grows.
3. Have faith that God loves you and blesses you every day.
4. Do something every day to help someone else!

The title of this book is *"Lucky 13"*, and that's me! I have been incredibly blessed in my life:

- I was raised by two of the best people I know, who showed me their love every day in countless ways.
- As they say, "I outkicked my coverage" when I married Debbie! She's a blessing to me every day—although I probably drive her crazy! I am truly blessed.
- My three children—Jesse, John, and Anna—are fantastic human beings. I couldn't be prouder of the

people they've become. Jesse's wife, Jennifer, John's wife, Carol, and Anna's husband, Ben are blessings to each of them, as well as to Debbie and me.

• My Grandkids:

o   Cataleya is our first grandchild, and she's especially close to Debbie and me. She has an amazing outlook on life and will one day be the greatest party planner ever!
o Hadley is a wonderful 8-year-old. She is full of life and gifted in everything she does. She's a delight to everyone.

o   Henry is so smart, so loud, and so much fun! His motor never stops running, and someday, I'll get him to eat vegetables!

o   Corinne, the third of the "Nashville crew," is really developing her own personality at 4 years old. What a sweet and bright young person—she's a joy! I've watched her blossom over the past year, and I can't wait to see her grow.

o   Gabriel and Genevieve, the two-year-old twins, bring endless blessings! God blessed Anna and her husband, Ben, with two dynamos. I can't get enough of them! Genevieve is effusive and constantly talking, while Gabriel is a little more reserved but equally hilarious. The two of them play off each other and are so much fun!

As you can tell, I am incredibly blessed. God has given me a life filled with wonderful family and friends. These blessings, along with my faith in God's grace, give me hope for the future.

The title of this chapter says it all: *Blessings + Faith = Hope*.

Because I have faith in God, I trust that He will continue to show me His blessings, and that gives me hope for future generations—and for you. Every morning, wake up, smile, and count how grateful you are for the opportunity to learn new things, meet new people, and make a difference in someone's life today. Along the way, SHOW UP, LOOK PEOPLE IN THE EYE, FIND OUT WHAT YOU'RE PASSIONATE ABOUT, AND GO FOR IT. EAT REAL FOOD (NOT PROCESSED), AND KEEP MOVING EVERY DAY.

I believe in the younger generation and their ability to grow and treat one another as they would want to be treated. We all face difficulties in life, and how you handle them will determine your ultimate success. You can do it— lean on the strength of the Lord and His love for you.

"You may not always have a comfortable life, and you will not always be able to solve all of the world's problems at once, but don't ever underestimate the impact you can have. History has shown us that courage can be contagious, and hope can take on a life of its own."
— Michelle Obama

Chapter 13 Food for Thought

- **<u>Chapter 13 Challenge</u>:**

____

____

____

- Express something in the last week that has given you hope for the future:

____

____

____

- Re-read Isaiah 40:31 above. How can you use this verse in your daily life?

____

____

____

- How are you blessed in your life?

____

____

____

*****

CONCLUSION

I want to share the words from a song I heard on our local Christian station the other day. The name of the song is, "Love Anyway", and is written by Drew & Ellie Holcomb. Their words draw the perfect conclusion to this book:

"When all your hopes are shattered

and you feel like your soul is a sea

Your dreams don't seem to matter

Your heart is bruised and battered

You can't feel anything

Love anyway-Love anyway

When your world has gone to hell

No story left to tell

Love anyway"

9 781966 131687